....face down and very dead!

Everett and Ann Colby

iUniverse, Inc.
New York   Bloomington

iUniverse books may be ordered through booksellers or by contacting:

iUniverse
1663 Liberty Drive
Bloomington, IN 47403
www.iuniverse.com
1-800-Authors (1-800-288-4677)

Because of the dynamic nature of the Internet, any Web addresses or links contained in this book may have changed since publication and may no longer be valid. The views expressed in this work are solely those of the author and do not necessarily reflect the views of the publisher, and the publisher hereby disclaims any responsibility for them.

ISBN: 978-1-4502-6285-9 (sc)
ISBN: 978-1-4502-6284-2 (ebook)

Printed in the United States of America

iUniverse rev. date: 1/14/2011

To Charles, Everett, Page, and Dianna

It's Done!

AUTHOR'S NOTE

The public generally agrees, as do I, that _traditional mysteries_ such as this are books best typified by the works of Agatha Christie. The genre is loosely defined as mysteries which contain no explicit sex or excessive gore or violence; and usually they feature an amateur detective, a confined setting and characters who know each other. What we can most certainly experience are lies, misunderstandings and denials, jealousy and revenge; a host of emotions. In this tale several of the people are real, yet certain fictionalized characterizations were developed due entirely to the author's very fertile imagination.

In this genre the actual murder is given limited attention. The true focus of the mystery involves the shattered relationships between the victim and those around him. The detective, whoever that turns out to be, seeks to find out what caused the turmoil in these lives. The emotions stemming from these broken relationships tend to impair the lives of every person involved.

So dear reader, the tale awaits you. Ultimately it is how these mangled emotions affect, and in many cases destroy ordinary lives, that engages us.

Contents

PROLOGUE

I've already been up for some time. I treasure these early morning hours, at our bed and breakfast, *Polite Society*, while our guests are still asleep or are beginning to rouse after what we hope was a very restful and pleasant night. I have set the breakfast table and the downstairs common rooms have been 'picked up'. Around this time the sun is just about rising over the tops of the ancient oak trees and beginning to creep ever so gently into the guest rooms facing east; and it is practically dancing into the dining room. There was no way I could know or be prepared for the devastating event later this day.

A well received morning ritual is the placing of freshly brewed special blend hazelnut coffee on the hallway table upstairs for guest enjoyment prior to them getting dressed and coming downstairs for breakfast. The captivating aroma slips into each room to tease the guests awake. I also lay out our local newspaper and the *Wall Street Journal* on the entry table, and in cooler seasons light welcoming fires in both the parlor and den. All of this; and the soft strains of Emile Pandolfi at the piano coming from the stereo. Doesn't everyone wake up for breakfast in this way?

"Good morning folks, it's a beautiful morning, … sure and it's just another day in paradise!" I take real pleasure in this little daily ritual. Each morning, as it approached 8:30AM and I heard the sound of footsteps on the stairs, I proudly positioned myself near the bottom step for this predictable greeting. It has been emphasized to everyone that breakfast is served at 8:30 sharp. Gently herding the folks toward the dining room they quickly sense the setting for a captivating event. "Wow, will you look at this"; and "Oh, my"; are typical reactions. The sun dazzles off the imposing 3 tier brass chandelier and the Waterford crystal's many faceted Lismore pattern. My mother's antique gold patterned wedding china and silver service compliment and complete the wonderful scene. *Polite Society* is … *a special place.*

Thus, with the stage set, the players in place…it is now what I like to call "SHOW TIME"!

As our brochure states, breakfast is a special time at *Polite Society,* a time for guests to make new friends, share personal experiences or adventures in Asheville, or simply just enjoy the wonderful food. Today, as is the norm, the time goes by pleasantly and effortlessly for all.

"Welcome to you all again," I repeat, "even though two of our guests apparently have decided to sleep in. I should mention that most guests find the personal service at breakfast, by yours truly, to be impeccable and quite concerned. Ahem!"

With this ever so subtle prodding on my part, our guests on some mornings have been moved to a standing ovation. Very nice!

Not once in the three years that we have enjoyed our life here as innkeepers, have I ever imagined that anything could possibly shatter this idyllic setting…. that is, until that fateful early summer morning when Horace Tydings wound up in our ornamental koi pond, *face down and very dead*!

CHAPTER I

The koi pond...

Thursday 9:30 AM

Asheville, North Carolina, ...After what now seemed like an eternity in our former lives when Chris and I both worked and commuted in New York City and then Miami, this little jewel of a city, snuggled in and surrounded by the gentle Blue Ridge Mountains, was unquestionably the end of the line for us.

"You want to do what? You want to go where?" I remember the conversations vividly. Both Chris and I were at the top of our respective games, so to speak: she was in charge of a merger and acquisitions department at her bank devoted to absorbing and successfully merging the operations of acquired banks; I was managing the corporate banking activities in Miami for the largest bank in Florida. Life was good. Yet I knew there was something more, and a burnout syndrome had already begun to invade my thoughts.

When I originally suggested this dramatic lifestyle change to Chris – of "dropping out" of corporate life to become innkeepers – and then presented a property to her that I had researched, she was at first highly amused, then incredulous when she realized that I was serious. She was subsequently moved to tears and ultimately became dangerously close to mutinous. Not for nothing had my choice of this nearly one hundred year old house been dubbed "the Amityville Horror" by the neighbors. Well, we each retired; Chris with great fanfare and many good wishes for success blended with hugs and tears from those who hated to see her leave, and I much more quietly.

Today, Chris and I are certain that we couldn't be any happier. Enormous satisfaction came from seeing what we created here; a total property restoration which was more costly than originally budgeted – of course – and which ultimately turned out just as we planned. It was almost scary how well things went.

We were usually very quick to point out to all inquirers that "now that we have found Asheville, we don't want anyone else to move here." We loved its 'small city' charm, and didn't want it to change its character with large growth. There was a kind of magnetism here, if you will, not unlike Paris or for that matter New York City. Right now in Asheville there was unquestionably an extremely strong generational pull. It was a place to love; it was a place to be contented.

Our bed and breakfast, *Polite Society,* is located in the Montford section of Asheville, an official Historic District. Along with our Dutch Colonial there are numerous stately old Victorian and Arts and Crafts homes in the district, many of which saw better times. The neighborhood is undergoing an aggressive gentrification process, which has predictably been a painful period for some, but a welcome breath of fresh air and godsend for most.

Today our inn is generally and aptly described as "a Special Place". We have enjoyed several complimentary newspaper and magazine articles from a number of travel writers. We are in many travel guides, and our success includes the envious and sought after goal of a significant number of return guests.

Most of our return guests avoided this upcoming weekend. Bele Chere was about to play out to an approximate five hundred thousand tourists and party-goers. This was the biggest tourist weekend of the year, and we had a full house. This morning's breakfast was concluded; as I glanced at the empty parking area I knew the guests had already departed for a day's activities. Well, maybe the loud obnoxious couple that checked in very late last night, and did not appear at breakfast might still be in their room. Forgive me Chris, but I couldn't care less. It was now what I called "my time".

I headed for the front gardens with a mug of hazelnut coffee, today's newspaper's crossword puzzle and my first Monte Cristo cigar of the day. One luxury this retired banker continued to guard jealousy was a premium cigar, but only outside, if you please. There was no smoking in the inn: 'no how, no way, not ever'. Chris placed pretty ceramic NO SMOKING signs throughout the inn. This policy was amply explained in our brochures, guide book listings and during the initial reservation process so there should be no misunderstandings at check-in.

I loved to watch as the morning's sunlight chased its own shadow across the face of the old inn. I never got tired of sitting, while more often than not simply day dreaming, in any one of my many favorite spots in the gardens. At the outset of the renovation process of this old property Chris and I spent considerable time poring over various historical references at the local library studying local gardens of the early twentieth century. In particular our gardens that faced the front street, as well as those on the side street, with both sun and shade, had been meticulously planned in this fashion. The use of hydrangeas with their brilliant, large blue faces, the purple flowering lilac bushes, the old reliable green and white hostas and the sweet smelling wisteria and honeysuckle were purposely meant to take one back in time to grandma's house. Blue forget-me-nots peeked out along the edges of the lawn. Another part of the gardens sported masses of lemon lilies, the tall flag-like spikes of delphiniums and purple cone flowers, all punctuated by the crisp white petals of Shasta daisies which were a particular favorite of Chris'. The front and side of the property, which was elevated and gave a commanding view from our corner lot was surrounded, and very well defined by a gleaming white picket fence which I designed myself, and spent considerable time explaining to our fencing contractor. Finally, completing this picture were several stately oaks and pleasant maples that provided a shady canopy over the walkway from the parking area in the rear to the front door. They were an absolute delight in the summer, but a mixed blessing in the fall when the abundance of leaves made a colorful patchwork quilt on the lawn that had to be raked and bagged daily by yours truly.

The gardens were a magnet, not only for guests, but for passers-by as well who looked up from the sidewalk through the fence at the profusion of colors. It was inviting enough for them simply to climb the steps from the sidewalk to get a better look over the top of the picket fence. The local tourist trolley stopped on occasion and that large group could actually be a real annoyance. My thoughts on this were simple, if you wanted to see the gardens, rent a room, and be a guest. I thought it, I didn't actually say it.

My reverie was suddenly broken by a loud splash from in the back, behind the library. I knew that sound! I quickly raced up the side porch steps, across the porch and down the other side to the koi pond. I was finally going to catch the neighbor's dog that had twice before set the pond's gold, orange and black and white koi into swirling panic. The race to the back took less than a dozen seconds.

I was momentarily stunned by what I saw. The huge form in the pond was not moving, and it was not a dog that I saw. Reacting instinctively, I grabbed the collar of the jacket on the half submerged body, and with some difficulty heaved the wet, dead weight onto the stone pathway.

I rolled the body onto its back, and stepped back in distress. Horace Tydings stared up at me with unseeing eyes and with a large angry bruise on the left side of his face. I turned away, unable to keep from gagging. I looked around the entire back garden, a cool, shady, and quietly green companion to the riot of color in the front, and then back to Tydings' face. I looked up again. There was no one in sight, no cars in the parking area, no one walking down the side or rear street, no cars going by. The other couples left right after breakfast for a day at our major tourist attraction, the Biltmore House. I quickly recovered, and felt his wrist for a pulse. I felt nothing. I tried for a pulse in the flaccid neck. Again, nothing! What I really wanted to do was get back out front as fast as I could and let someone else come across this grotesque body. No! No good! His body was already out of the pond. I simply couldn't stand here like an idiot and do nothing. I began shouting for Chris to call 911. I told her to report an accident. It didn't occur to me that it could be anything else.

I watched Chris react to the tone in my voice as she grabbed the phone and dialed 911 as she raced down the library steps toward me.

"What happened?" Chris's voice was clear and firm. She was a rock in any emergency. Chris was an in-charge lady, not one to be described as saccharine or bland and certainly not easily frightened. Her reactions always came after the crisis was handled.

"Listen to me, Chris. I was sitting out front, and I heard this splash. I thought it was that dammed dog again. This is what I found in the pond instead!"

Chris was on the phone with the 911 operator: "Hello, 911, this is Chris Loving. We have urgent need for medical help. There has been a very serious fall into a pond on our property. The address is the *Polite Society* bed and breakfast at the corner of Pearson Drive and Tacoma Circle. The person does not appear to be breathing."

She received the 911 acknowledgement and looked at me with dismay and more that a little concern. I could tell that a fast-forward of events was playing out in her mind.

"Don't look at me, I didn't do anything. I was enjoying my morning cigar out front when I heard a splash back here. All I did was to pull him out of the pond."

I couldn't help but blurt out what I was really thinking.

"This is just great! Here we are, the inn's full, it's the best weekend of the summer with an otherwise great group of guests, and this clumsy s.o.b. does a 'brodie' into the pond." I was immediately chagrined at my reaction. But this was more than an intrusion or an irritant, if you will. I certainly couldn't continue to share these thoughts out loud.

I looked at Chris, and since in times of stress my wise-guy comes out I said: "Say babe, what was that line in *The Godfather?* Sleeping with the fishes?"

"Ed, please, don't be obnoxious, and for goodness sake, watch what you say."

Chris looked around at the uneven stepping stones around the pond. She had asked me on several occasions to 'fix' this path, to smooth out the walkway because of the possibility of someone tripping; but to tell the truth, I had not paid attention. I thought the 'been there forever' look of the slightly uneven stones, (and dammed, they were only *slightly* uneven) added to the ambiance…but now *this*.

Another slightly paranoid thought struck me. Horace Tydings probably did this on purpose, to make a case to sue me! I should never have let him check in last night. I knew he would only come to my place to cause trouble.

He had been his usual overly arrogant self last night, as I manfully acted the part of a gracious host to this surprise and unwelcome 'guest'. Naturally he arrived with some fanfare, the rented stretch Mercedes limo taking up one lane of the street out front. Adding to this grand entrance he made sure I knew he arrived at the Asheville airport in his new 244DM Challenger, a Canadian-built private jet which seats maybe 8-12, capable of flying from New York to Paris non-stop in incomparable luxury. The cost, he told me was somewhere around twenty to twenty five *million* dollars. I bet he probably acquired it from one of the many hapless companies he'd raided and fleeced, leaving the majority of employees jobless.

Bringing myself back to the present 'situation' I took several deep breaths to help me calm down.

I noticed Felicia, our phlegmatic and overweight Maine Coon Cat, sitting regally posed, at the edge of the rose garden overlooking the koi pond. Until the move to Asheville, Felicia was strictly a house cat for the eight years she's lived in Miami. These days she often sat here in the garden for long periods of time, staring at the birds flocking to the feeders nearby, as well as at the koi gliding about in the pond. Some instinct told her that she should be doing something about them all, but so far she hadn't, and my guess was that she never would. Now I wondered how long had she's been sitting there and did she witness the accident?

"Talk to me cat, tell me what happened here. There you sit with that typical imperious cat look. You know something, but you can't tell me anything."

I turned away from Felicia and in growing frustration asked Chris "What do we do now with this stiff?"

"For crying out loud, Ed, you must watch what you say. I know you're nervous, but this could turn into an ugly situation."

"This mutt is the only ugly thing around here. I could swear he has a smirk on his face! Truthfully he really doesn't look too good, but then he never did!"

"Stay calm, honey," Chris said this as if it was an order. "Calm yourself down and let's just wait for the emergency folks."

The crunching of tires on the graveled parking area attracted us both.

Chris ran up to first responders, two men from the Asheville Fire Department. On their heels came the ambulance with the EMTs in their dark blue jumpsuits, carrying their bright orange canisters, looking quite business-like.

"Over here, please, next to the pond. One of our guests seems to have fallen into the koi pond. My husband heard the splash and pulled him out, but he looks awful."

They sized up the situation quickly; in fact one of the EMTs was already stooping over Tydings, pulling on gloves while making a survey of the body. We knew that despite a zero to minimal pulse the EMTs would do all in their power to resuscitate the victim. Both were now busy with the body. Chris and I just stood here. After a few minutes one of them stood up and looked straight at me.

"It appears that this man received a blow to the face or hit his head on one of these rocks. It could have knocked him out. He's not breathing on his own, and it doesn't look good." He turned to the other EMT. "Joe, bring the respirator here."

One of the firemen approached me. "Tell me what happened here."

I recounted again the series of events. As I told the story I began to feel a strong sense of unease and nervousness.

"I'm not sure just how this accident happened. I was out front taking my usual after breakfast break when I heard a splash in the pond. I believed that all of the guests had left. I certainly did not expect to find one of my guests face down among the lily pads and fish. My guess is that he tripped somehow. I actually thought the disturbance was made by a neighborhood dog."

I carefully went over the details of where I found Tydings, how I'd pulled him out of the pond and that I didn't feel a pulse. I recounted the time element and the call to 911 when I realized there was a person in the pond.

After seeming to digest this, the fireman asked in a flat voice, "And how do *you* think he got that bruise on the side of his face?"

That ticked me off. Too quickly I replied. "I don't know. He must have hit the rocks around the edge of the pond when he fell. How the hell should I know?"

Pulling the radio off his belt he told the dispatcher in no uncertain terms: "You better call for police to follow up on the call to *Polite Society,* the bed and breakfast on Pearson Drive in Montford." Getting a nod from the EMT, he continued "We have a DB on the premises, can't raise a pulse."

I know DB stood for dead body.

Turning to Chris and me he said "He's already got a bruise but according to what you just said, you heard the splash as he fell into the pond at most ten minutes ago, say 10:10. Something's fishy here." We all started at this unintended pun. My anxiety level rose faster. I knew this accident was starting to look like something else entirely, and I knew where they would look first when our past history came to light.

Just then an additional vehicle pulled into the parking area, and a man stepped out of a white car with the skyline of Asheville decoratively painted inside the outlines of the letters that spelled POLICE. Recognizing the new arrival, the Fireman thumbed the switch on his radio. "Forget the last call. Officer is now on the scene."

I too recognized the new arrival. It was Lieutenant Richard Davis, a neighborhood guy and the last person I wanted looking into something that happened on my property.

"Hey Ed, how ya doing. I was just on my way home for an early lunch; saw the ambulance, and wondered if I could help. What have you got here?"

At this he removed a well chewed toothpick from his lips. Gee, I thought, but didn't offer, toothpicks were generally used after one ate.

Who I had here, I knew, was the lead detective for our fair city; perhaps the number three man in the department. Lieutenant Davis looked more like a street person. His unruly mop of brown unkempt hair was the result of continuous poor haircuts. His wife probably put a bowl over the curls and cuts around the edge I thought to myself. To make matters worse, he kept pushing back his straying forelock as if this were proper, and improved his appearance. His dirty wrinkled raincoat, totally unnecessary on such a beautiful warm sunny day only added to his overall sartorial splendor - not! He even stood with one hand holding his bent elbow, just like the famous TV icon, Colombo, analyzing the situation. His little dime store cigars were part of the overall copycat look; his faded black and blue flannel shirt and blue knit tie were a departure from the original, as was his ever present plastic pocket protector, stuffed with pens. His faded and baggy corduroy pants were a perfect accompaniment. I couldn't imagine that those pants were ever introduced to an iron. What a prize! And folks, he was all ours!

Before I could reply, the fireman gave the lieutenant a quizzical look. "We responded to a slip and fall accident here, but this man's face looks like somebody was pretty deliberate. It also looks to me like it happened a lot earlier than 911 got the call."

Lieutenant Davis knelt by the body for some time, and looked carefully at the pond. I saw that he has put on latex gloves and was moving around quite deliberately.

"What about Tydings' wife?"

Leave it to Chris to think of what other complications would arise. "Could she still be upstairs, in their room with all this commotion going on at the back of the house?"

Chris and I pondered this as we respectfully stood off to one side away from the flurry of activity.

"One thing at a time, Chris. I see Lieutenant Davis heading for us, and he doesn't look too neighborly."

Lieutenant Davis pulled me aside. "Now I know you've already spoken to the EMTs about what happened here, but I don't like the looks of that mark on the victim's face at all. In fact, I find it highly suspicious and my immediate thought is that it's inconsistent with an accidental fall into the fishpond. I am sorry to do this, but I am going to lock down and seal the entire back yard as a possible crime scene. I hate to do this Mr. and Mrs. Loving, but I really don't like what I see here. Could one of your guests have done this?"

I was completely dumbfounded. And more that a little worried.

"Excuse me a minute, Mr. Loving. I've got to call in the necessary personnel."

I knew it! I turned to Chris. "The lieutenant is taking a distinct pleasure in all this. He jumps to his conclusions pretty fast, doesn't he? You recognize him, don't you? He's the one who is so active in this historic district neighborhood. Remember, he kept saying he was born here, and grew up here and the local people should have the most say in what happens here."

Chris slowly nodded her head, as if calling up a memory. She had been angrier than I was at the difficulty we had with the historic society in getting permission for some of the renovations we wanted to do. Ironically, a number of these had to do with making the property safer for our guests.

"He's in a position of importance in the city. There are Davis's throughout the city, and they all seem to be related in some way. So many of them look alike too. I know that he, along with several other neighbors resent the 'invasion' of 'outsiders' who are buying up and renovating a number of these older houses. You know yourself Chris that they particularly resent the 'B&B people' as they call us."

Chris and I both knew that we were not really accepted as true participants in the gentrification of this wonderful old neighborhood; rather we are viewed as being here simply to make a buck in a short time period and then get out. A more serious criticism, and this was a major bone of contention, was that the renovation of these grand old properties increased the assessed valuation of the surrounding houses, thus increasing their property taxes. This was understandably tough on the older and longer term homeowners. Of course many of these same people were annoyed that a bed and breakfast might bring increased traffic throughout the neighboring streets, particularly on the weekends.

"No, Chris, I don't think we can consider Lieutenant Davis an ally at this point. I bet, although I hope I'm wrong, that he'll go out of this way to make things as difficult for us and our guests as possible. He's coming back now after setting in motion a major and unnecessary brouhaha."

"All right Mr. Loving, I have several uniforms coming who will seal off and comb the immediate area, as well as conduct a neighborhood canvass, perhaps of a square block. Also, my forensic team will be here shortly. In the meantime I've asked a woman sergeant to come here to accompany Mrs. Tydings to Mission Hospital once I've asked her a few questions. Her husband will be taken there. We'll need her to make a positive ID."

Just then we heard a commotion up stairs… "What're you saying, what, what, what?"

We couldn't make out everything being said, but certainly we heard some of the slurred words, even a few Spanish phrases that I know were not pleasant idioms. This get - away weekend had not turned out so well for our Latin bombshell who had checked in last night with Tydings. I looked up at the window in the hallway but couldn't see a thing. Apparently Lieutenant Davis' sergeant had arrived and successfully met the Latin hurricane upstairs; the sooner she was gone the better. We certainly didn't need a returning guest to experience her expletives. 'What else?' I thought.

Lieutenant Davis hadn't yet met this woman who represented herself as Tydings' wife. "What was that?" he asked.

"What was what?" Chris asked, straight-faced.

"Come on, you two, who is that upstairs? Is that this man's wife?"

Chris and I had the very same instant thought 'you really don't want to know'. Keeping our thoughts to ourselves, we two just looked at him, extended our palms and shrugged our shoulders. I said "Why Lieutenant, that's the supposed Mrs. Tydings. At least that's how she was represented to me last night. My wife hasn't had the pleasure yet."

The Lieutenant gave us a hard look. "I'll be here for some time, and as soon as possible, I'll sit down with you. I want to go over with both of you, very carefully, the series of events that occurred here."

I didn't like the sound of that nor of what I sensed as the apparent pleasure Davis took in trampling all over our property; particularly as he's designated it a crime scene. I also didn't like the sickly sweet smell of his cheap cigars. And, of course, the longer he stayed here, the more of the plastic tips from these cigars would appear in my private ashtray by the kitchen steps. I hated to think any guest might think that I smoked those horrors.

Chris gave me a concerned look, noted my frustration, and nodded her head.

"Lieutenant, we'll be right here when you want us. It goes without saying that we want this tragic episode cleared up as soon as possible. We're not going anywhere. Just knock on the kitchen door. One of us is never very far from the kitchen."

Turning to me, she said "Let's go inside. You can't stand here and watch his men draping that horrid yellow tape all over the place. In a few minutes this will look like the last place you want to be. We need to talk, and gather our wits about us."

Sitting in the kitchen, Chris was pensive. The morning's events had gotten to her. She sat there looking so sad and she seemed to stare right through me. I was quiet as well, absently rubbing my thumb against the adjoining two fingers. Then Chris focused on me.

"What are you thinking right now? Tell me! I must admit that this move to Asheville wasn't high on my list of things to do, but until now, it has gone wonderfully well for us. We really are very happy in this little town. You've been so revitalized. I didn't realize just how restless you were in Miami. This move has been like an elixir for you, Ed. That curt banker who rarely smiled has been replaced by a very pleasant fellow. Your old friends in Miami wouldn't believe it; at least not the ones who haven't been here yet. Those buddies of yours who have come up to stay, or just visited, can't believe how different you are. They so enjoy the 'new' you. As your Brooklyn bar buddies would say, 'you're a regular prince!' At the bank you clearly had a tendency to be pompous, but now you're more the comfortable cardigan clad type one expects to find as the host of a bed and breakfast. And you made all this success happen. It was you who found this place and planned the move. You researched the bed and breakfast business, and developed solid business and marketing plans. You threw yourself into the start up problems of a small business. I love your renewed enthusiasm. It's been like your first big move to executive management, when you thought you could make changes for the better."

With a catch in her throat she continued talking earnestly to me.

"Ed, I now realize that this accident could be a really bad experience, for us and the business. But we can't let it take away from us all we've accomplished so far. Look at you: tanned, trim and happy with yourself and our life now. Every thing is going so well, except for your dammed cigars! We know we don't have anything to do with Mr. Tydings' accident. And pretty soon so will Lieutenant Davis. We'll work through this, get our world back in focus, and get on with our wonderful life. We'll continue taking good care of our guests, too. This is something so weird; it just can't have anything to do with us. We'll fix it, honey!"

"We can get some help in that." I replied. "I should call our attorney, Dan, right now".

"No, not yet, Ed. It has to be an accident. Let's see where our meeting with Lieutenant Davis takes us. We can stop that at any time if the situation looks compromising."

Chris grew silent. I realized she has quickly grasped the seriousness of what happened. She had just gotten a lot off her chest, and looked for my reaction. I wondered what she feared most. She was quite in tune with Lieutenant Davis, his supposed requirements and most importantly, the seriousness of the situation.

As for me, several concerns now raced through my mind. I worried about how the remaining guests are going to react to all this, and whether they will want to leave immediately. How long will that yellow crime scene tape be fluttering in the breeze, making a mockery of our slogan… 'A Special Place'? Everything in the near future was in total confusion. Would we still prepare the planned fundraising brunch for one of our favorite charities, the Asheville Symphony Guild? That always had a good turnout and raised significant monies. Will we now be shunned, and only the gawking curious want to come poking about asking rude questions? We could be dropped from the Asheville Holiday Tour of Homes, too. And what about our own family reunion scheduled here later this summer? On and on, the doubts and questions ran. But most importantly my mind kept going back to 'what really did happen here, and how could I have missed it?' I was there just seconds after I heard the big splash, and there was absolutely no one in sight. It had to have been an accident, and Tydings own fault.

How strange, how very strange.

CHAPTER II

Horace Tydings….

Thursday, 12 Noon

I watched from the kitchen window as the various jump-suited technicians went back-and-forth over the accident scene. To the untrained eye, it might seem like chaos, but it was a trained team doing its thing. The fingerprint team scanned and dusted; the hair and fiber team scrutinized every surface, the serology team scraped and the coroner's team sniffed. From the sidelines the videographers recorded everything. What a show; a regular three ring circus, albeit a very serious circus! And soon the detective's interrogation.

The accident scene had already been trampled on by me and Chris, and then the paramedics. Several tooth picks and cigar butts were lying about at the edges; not 'policed' by the good Lieutenant. It was a wonder with all that traffic that any forensic evidence had a degree of integrity.

"Here we have a house full of guests; the other three couples, at this point, are totally unaware of the accident, and they haven't even met the Tydings couple, to boot. It still escapes me that our prize couple didn't bother to come down for breakfast this morning. Probably they didn't want to mix with the 'common people'. Why did they come to our bed and breakfast, or any other bed and breakfast for that matter? From my experience Tydings was strictly a flashy resort type, where he enjoyed people bowing and scraping to him. I just can't understand it. Why did they come here? Unless, he expected me to cater to him and to bow and scrape. Fat chance!"

I was getting myself agitated. Chris was well aware of my highly protective stance of what all this would mean to the other guests, and more particularly to our prized inn. She also knew that I had an unusually strong dislike of men such as Tydings. Even so, she was truly surprised that I was so uncharacteristically rigid in my opinion of Tydings.

"I knew we were in for trouble when Tydings checked in with that over-made up bimbo last night. I knew damn well she was not his wife."

Chris just rolled her eyes at me. Thinking back, I remembered now that it was 'Mrs. Tydings' who made the reservations, and that she made the reservations under the name 'Ms. Greene', party of two.

Chris jumped in, "Now, honey, don't get all excited until we get a final determination from Lieutenant Davis. This could very well be just as we originally thought; a terrible accident. Then, maybe, Ms. Greene, or Mrs. Tydings, or whoever she is, will simply check out and be done with us. At the risk of getting you all excited again, Mr. Innkeeper, tell me, just what it is about Tydings that brings out the worst in you? I've never seen you act like this about any other guest, or for that matter, anyone else at all. I know there is some kind of history here between you two that goes back to Miami. But I thought that you never did any business with him. Please, can you calm down and tell me what it is."

"Oh, it's a lot of things. It is not unusual at all to meet many obnoxious businessmen when you're in a position at the bank to lend large sums of money, as I was. But there was universal agreement among lenders everywhere that a very special description be reserved for the worst of the worst; the term is 'beast', and that my dear describes Horace Tydings to a 'T'."

"Described." corrected Chris.

Getting myself all wound up again I didn't even notice the correction.

"In a nutshell his particular 'style' was to acquire control of a company, perhaps one that was having more than a little spot of trouble, and then, with his controlling interest, suck whatever cash there was out through outrageous levels of compensation. There were too many examples of his companies throughout the country that were simply pressured into bankruptcy; then sold off in pieces to the highest bidders. Horace Tydings' disgraceful treatment of the people trapped in his acquisitions was legion. He had little regard for sacrificing the remaining personnel of acquired companies, usually through firings, not to mention the owners who fared poorly as well. Hell, I lost count after the first two, the number of owners who either committed suicide or lost all respect for themselves and entered deep depressions after realizing what happened to their company and loyal employees after the acquisition papers were finalized; and this was just in Florida. As far as Mr. Tydings and I are concerned, he knew that I was vehemently opposed to "Greenmail", at which he excelled. He never got our bank to support him as long as I was in charge of the bank's corporate lending activities. Quite simply his method was to have a bank lend him the necessary funds to accumulate a large enough percentage of a particular company's outstanding stock, either in the open market or direct from private investors."

"Tydings' army of well paid analysts was primed to tell him which companies appeared to be ripe for take-over. The beauty for Tydings was that he bought before any other offer was announced; that's where the real juice was in the take-over game. First one in before the problems became public knowledge."

"Tell me", Chris interrupted me, "how he could do that; it's got to be tough to hit on deals where you buy stock even before the first offer, to my way of thinking. You'd have to have privileged information to do it with any consistency."

I couldn't help the sarcasm that crept into my voice "What you mean is *insider* information, and my dear, trading on insider information is illegal. Tydings has been at the center of several SEC investigations because of this, but with much winking and blinking and nodding he has generally stayed clear of any indictable violations. He claims his army of analysts provides him with perfectly legal information. Once in a while it happened that owners were embarrassed by their financial problems and erroneously saw that beast as a white knight. They certainly learned differently as soon as the ink was dry. Regardless, Tydings reputation was far from pristine. "

"This activity can be hypnotic, Chris. Rational people blinded by the fees and extraordinary profits. Greed! That's what Tydings and his people counted on! There were several nice little plums throughout

Florida that he would have loved to move on, with our support, but he knew I never would support him by lending him the money to make his move. He didn't like me; and I thought that he was slime-ball."

Chris got a thoughtful look and asked simply, "Why didn't he just go to another bank? Why did he keep coming back to you? I'm sure he knew other banks and bankers. Why not go to them first, and avoid you completely?"

"Well, that was certainly a question I asked myself early on; particularly since I knew that he did business with some large New York City banks. They may have had a credit limit with him, or God forbid, maybe they likewise were adverse to his manipulations. No, the best answer I could ever manage was that because we were Florida's home grown bank, the largest state institution, and enjoyed a wonderful reputation we would bring all that to the table if we partnered with Tydings. He could feed off our good reputation when needed. No thanks! By the same token, because of our pre-eminent position in Florida, if we were not involved it raised some questions, and a degree of apprehension for other lenders. You may recall that I even had a few directors who questioned my motives. They had very craftily been retained by Tydings for various activities, and Tydings paid well, knowing full well the power of the buck. As they say: 'So much, for the independence of outside directors'. God, I am so happy to be out of that situation."

"I'm sorry to run on like this, Chris, honey, but this guy belonged........ well, he really belonged behind bars, but that won't happen now. In a way I found him to be a laughable study, a complete turn-off, he with his little Napoleon complex. I'll never forget how he'd show up at the bank, with his few remaining hairs grown to an absurd length, pomaded and plastered over his shining dome. I swear he even had makeup on his face. His nails were polished, not just buffed; and his shoes, he must have had them built up at least three inches. To complete this lovely portrait, he would have a fresh carnation in his lapel, and yeah, his jewelry was also tasteless, the gold Rolex, the huge pinkie diamond, and enormous black onyx cuff links for his French cuffs. What a package."

Suddenly I was feeling very drained. I needed to change topics, and fast. I had to get off this subject. In an attempt to lighten the mood, I brought up a whole new subject.

"What do you think, dear, will this entire mess greatly affect my play at the Club's annual member-member golf tournament this weekend?"

Chris nearly shrieked. "Are you serious? You can't leave me to take care of this all by myself." Her tone sobered. "I can tell that you are a little bit serious. Of course you can't play golf this coming weekend. Lord knows what it will be like here in the near future."

Dropping the topic of golf Chris continued with the next topic on her mind. "O.K. Let's plan to be ready when Lieutenant Davis comes back for his additional interviews. And, please, please don't continue to carry on so about Tydings. One could think you had a good motive to do him in."

The ringing phone broke the mood and Chris answered. "Polite Society, this is Chris, how may I help you?"

"Oh, hi Page. What's new? How are my grandchildren?"

Page is our daughter in Texas, and Chris was transformed and suddenly was wearing her 'mother' smile, the one that lighted up her whole face, and smoothed out the everyday stress lines. She became totally absorbed with our daughter, and all was right in her world. Page was named after my favorite aunt, and had done a fine job of supplying Chris and me with two grandchildren. Page had grown in a very short time into an accomplished business woman and quite adept at the marketing and promotions business. At least that was my opinion. I was fond of telling people that I spent the past twenty-five years trying to get rid of the four children we had, and now I was going to spend the next twenty-five years trying to get them back! They were now, truly, our best friends. Some wonderful and unexpected transformations took place after their college graduations and they all became what I call 'real people'. I always claimed that a mortgage would surely shake them to reality, and by golly it had. Some well managed debt had made us all come to some frightening uniformity in thinking. Clearly, I had gotten smarter as they had gotten older. Now, I wished they lived closer than Houston, Palm Beach, San Francisco, and Ottawa, Canada. Granted, nice places for us to visit, but not what you would call around the corner.

"I'm outta here," I said. "I have some calls to make. Say hello for me, and tell her I'll talk to her next week. Give the kids a hug for me. I'll use the private phone line downstairs in my office."

"Hold on, Ed! Page, repeat that, your father was trying to tell me something while you were talking." An unexpected silence followed. Chris' face changed. I knew that look. Something was wrong with one of her chicks. I could almost see her fluff up wings to spread them out over one of her brood. Great, something else was wrong!

"Oh, that's terrible Page. What will he do now? What about you, and the children, for heaven's sake? You can all come here. You need a vacation anyway. If you need any help with money, I'm sure the old skin-flint standing right here can be squeezed a little."

Now my attention is fully engaged. "What's going on? What happened?"

"Hold on again, honey; Dad's asking questions." Chris cupped her hand over the telephone. She turned to me. "Vince lost his job, well not lost it exactly, yet. The company had not been doing well for the past six months, ever since they were taken over by that conglomerate out of Miami." Suddenly Chris paled. "On my God, Ed, you don't think, I mean, would that be one of Tydings companies?"

"I wouldn't be a bit surprised!" I had forgotten all about that. I'll bet that's something Lieutenant Davis would find extremely interesting. "Tydings sure has been doing a job on this family today!"

I turned around to the kitchen window. Something caught the corner of my eye. Uh oh! I saw the good Lieutenant striding away from the back steps toward his car. How long had he been standing outside the window, hearing our conversations? Had we just given him something to think about, before he returned to talk to us?

Chris continued her conversation with Page. From the sound of things she didn't think this was the right time to tell Page of the day's events here at the inn. Poor kid, she's got her own full plate for awhile. I decided to go on down to my office and make some calls of a more serious nature. The golf tournament was of minor concern now. Clearly of more importance, I had to talk to a few folks in Miami, right away. When Lieutenant Davis came back I'd gladly find time to go over everything with him. It was now one o'clock. With a little luck I might get my calls made and still squeeze in a nap before the guests return from their day's activities.

In another part of town, on a totally different score, the events at Mission Hospital were not exactly what Sergeant Howe had expected.

The good sergeant had been on the Asheville police force for fourteen years and most of her experience had been in the administrative area. Chosen specifically by Lieutenant Davis to accompany "Mrs. Tydings" to the hospital she had been told by him in no uncertain terms that she was to be prepared to give comfort to, and be sensitive to 'Mrs.Tydings' needs. Perhaps more importantly, she was to be alert, and report back on any statement 'Mrs. Tydings' might make. Sergeant Howe, a good and kindly woman, a mother, grandmother, and long time resident of this mountain city was simply not prepared for - Ms. Daisy Martinez!

"I tell you, right now, right here; I'm no Mrs. Horace Tydings! On the head of my mother, I don't know him that good. We meet at the Jockey Club in Miami a few weeks ago and have a few drinks, a few laughs, you know? He takes me shopping; some clothes, some jewelry and then one day he says we're going on a little trip to the mountains. I say 'sure', why not."

Sergeant Howe wanted to describe Daisy as a small woman, but Daisy's head of thick luxurious black hair combined with black stiletto heels, made her appear taller than she was. The amount of material needed for what purported to be Ms. Martinez's black skirt - mini at best - would probably make only a pair of shorts for one of Sergeant Howe's grandchildren. Being 'poured' into a skirt was taking on a new meaning for Sergeant Howe. The too tight skirt was set off with an equally snug lemon yellow blouse with black polka dots and a pearl gray jacket. Surely not to be dismissed by anyone were her God-given and generously endowed physical attributes – Ahem! Daisy's necklace was crystal and pearl, very large beads. She wore chunky black earrings and a big bracelet of black and gray something. Her stockings were pale gray and had a small random flower pattern. She had a large black purse and a lavender overnight bag.

What a handful! She pranced back and forth in a well chosen, out of the way hospital waiting room, constantly lighting up long thin black papered cigarettes and completely ignoring the NO SMOKING sign, flicking ashes here and there. The sergeant thought better of trying to corral or challenge this woman .... better just to isolate her.

"I tell you again, I am Daisy Martinez, originally from West New York, and I been in Miami for two years. I do a little modeling, a little professional dancing, you know."

Sergeant Howe "knew" all too well about the true nature of the latter activity. There was little question that whatever veneer Ms. Martinez might have hoped to adopt to hide her Latin roots was now gone by the boards.

"Choo know what I mean? I don' wan to have nothing to do with anybody dying. And that doctor in there, he think this ain't no accident. What did he say, 'this is highly suspicious'! I heard him on the phone. I don' know from nothin' about anythin'. I jus' wanna get outta here, and get my stuff from that old house. That something else, everything in there so old! I don' like it. Let me get back to Miami!"

Sergeant Howe had learned that the medical examiner, a local doctor filling the function had refused to sign a Death Certificate, and had reported to Lieutenant Davis that indeed the head wound was suspicious. The body would be sent for a complete autopsy to the State Bureau of Investigation in Garner, North Carolina.

The one thing that Sergeant Howe did not know was what to do now with Ms. Daisy Martinez. The sergeant had already phoned in to headquarters a very lengthy report on what had transpired at the hospital to include being faithful and complete in reporting all of Daisy's statements. Now she would have to call Lieutenant Davis personally about the Latin Bombshell's desire to beat a hasty retreat from Asheville.

Horace Tydings had clearly managed to leave his mark on Asheville today.

CHAPTER III

Lieutenant Davis....

Thursday, 3:45 PM

It was mid-afternoon, closer to four o'clock when Lieutenant Davis knocked on the kitchen door. Chris was closer at hand. I watched her answer the door.

"Good afternoon Lieutenant, come in. May I get you some coffee or tea?"

"No thank you Mrs. Loving. I'm just fine." The lieutenant fingered his package of cigarillos.

"Lieutenant, may I remind you that there is no smoking inside the inn." Chris was polite but firm.

The lieutenant smiled his understanding. "That's why I've gone to chewing on toothpicks. I'm trying to stop smoking, but so far, no dice."

Chris looks fatigued by the events of the day. She had watched the parade in and out of the rear gardens for the past three hours or so. There were uniforms, plainclothes, technicians, a photographer, medical examiner, ambulance attendants; the neighbors at bay behind our fence; the cars slowing down to rubberneck at the activity had all been here. The shouts of "What happened? You're kidding! I don't believe it!" from the neighbors rang out now and then. --------- We are now two of the anonymous citizens whose lives have become defined by a simple roll of yellow crime scene tape. Surely word of what happened was now fanning out in the neighborhood, particularly by those officers going door to door on the immediate block.

"Before I talk to your husband, and I hope this is a good time for you both, maybe you can tell me your version of what happened this morning around the fish pond".

I heard Chris chuckle. "Lieutenant, are you using that very traditional police interviewing style, aimed at putting people at ease, but also seeing if there are significant differences in their stories? I don't mind talking to you alone at all Lieutenant and this is as good a time as there will be. As we already told you, around ten o'clock this morning I heard Ed shout from the koi pond to call 911; he was yelling that someone had fallen into the pond. Up until that time I had been busy here in the kitchen and then in the library. After hearing Ed's shouts for help, I grabbed the phone and raced down the library steps. I called in the accident, and asked 911 for medical help. Right away I saw that Ed had pulled someone from the pond. It was, I learned, Horace Tydings, a guest who had checked in the night before for a four day stay. And yes, there was no question about it. We couldn't help but notice the large red mark on Tydings cheek, spreading toward his eye."

As is invariably the case with the truth, it was easy for Chris to relate the events.

"Could you be more exact about what time this was?"

"Possibly", said Chris, "But better yet, just check your records of the incoming 911 calls, Lieutenant."

"You're so right, Mrs. Loving. You know I'm just doing my job. I think that's all for now, and if you don't mind, maybe you can call your husband. I hope he is of a mind to be helpful. I know he thinks I don't like 'the B&B people' in our neighborhood, but really that's not true. You both are professional in your dealings with your guests and pleasant to your neighbors, and I know Ed has gone out of his way to be a good sport in the neighborhood. I have to say his sponsorship of a Little League team this year was very well received. And Mrs. Loving, I know your seven layer cookies were a world class hit at the block party in the spring. You 'B&B folks' really are a credit to the neighborhood for restoring houses in this grand old neighborhood and populating them with good citizens. The 'gentrification process' as it's called, is not an easy one. It's hard to change peoples' minds and perceptions. But I must say we have come a long way."

"OK, so much for my speech and my soap box. I did want you to know that, and it will be helpful if we met each other halfway as professionals in this trying process. Suspicious accidents are just that, and are really no fun. You may not know this, but by law we have to treat them as homicides until proven otherwise."

Chris smiled at the sincerity of Davis' remarks. "Ed's downstairs in his office making calls, Lieutenant; just go on down and knock at his office door."

Davis descended the stairs, and saw the light on and the open door to my office. He knocked softly as I sat deep in thought. The lieutenant looked around and noticed the several plaques and proclamations on the wall for my charitable and civic involvement over the years, particularly in Miami. I thought that I could read his mind from the expressions on this face: this guy was really involved and surely well connected in his former life.

"Well, look at this", he said. "a letter from the Mayor of Miami recognizing your activities, and a gracious acknowledgment of the city's appreciation. Hey, what's this? This one really catches my interest."

Framed and hanging on the wall was the actual Honorable Discharge for a James B. Colby, 12th Regiment, New Hampshire Infantry Volunteers. The discharge was dated June 14, 1865.

"Wow," the Lieutenant said.

He nodded toward the Civil War discharge. "I'm quite proud of my military service." he said. "I was in Vietnam, and had seriously considered the military as a career. But the call of the mountains was just too much, and law enforcement seemed the next best thing. I think I made the right decision. All aspects military still interest me, though, especially the Civil War. Just recently I was asked to get involved in a re-enactment of a minor Civil War battle that took place near Asheville. You know, folks here in Asheville are not known for their parochial feelings about the Civil War ...and that's what it is called here, the Civil War. Not 'the war of northern aggression' or the 'war for southern independence' that other southern folks are disposed to call it. The War itself, and the plans for a re-enactment of a local battle, are simply an attempt by the local population to enjoy retelling a bit of the history of this wonderful area. No more. That's why a guy like me is very interested in getting involved."

Lieutenant Davis attempted to seem apologetic. I thought I knew what was behind his 'folksy' manner.

"Sorry to bother you down here, but Mrs. Loving said to come on down. I was struck by the many honors on the walls." His eyes continued to move from plaque to picture.

"That's just my little ego trip, Lieutenant. I come down here sometimes just to re-live some of those activities. Not many people ever come down here. In fact, as I look at these symbols of another life, I become more convinced each time that Chris and I are so fortunate to have found our little niche here in Asheville."

"Say, look at this one, what a hoot. Give me a sec; let me read a few lines." A framed poster titled *Capitalism for Dummies* had caught his eye.

<u>Traditional American Capitalism</u>: You have 2 cows: you sell one to buy a bull; your herd multiplies and the economy grows. You sell them and retire on the income.

<u>French Capitalism</u>: You have 2 cows: you go on strike because you want 3 cows.

<u>German Capitalism</u>: You have 2 cows: you re-engineer them so they live for 100 years, eat once a month and milk themselves.

<u>Italian Capitalism</u>: You have 2 cows: you don't know where they are. You break for lunch.

<u>British Capitalism</u>: You have 2 cows: both are mad.

<u>Chinese Capitalism:</u> You have 2 cows: you have 300 people milking them; you claim full employment, high economic activity, and arrest the man who reported the numbers.

<u>Irish Capitalism:</u> You have 2 cows: you feed them potatoes and wonder why they emigrate.

"That's really very funny, Mr. Loving. I envy your sense of humor and your wonderful experiences, too. You know Mr. Loving; I've had a little notoriety myself. My dad was a stock car driver here in Asheville, and after the track was closed down by the "elite" of the city, he worked on a NASCAR pit crew for Richard Petty.

I was interested now. "You mean King Richard?"

Lieutenant Davis nodded. "I was his protégé"

"What? No way! Get outta here."

"Yes, really. I had a great future. I was a "natural" I was told, and Petty was to be my mentor. It was all set up and then it all went to hell."

I was all ears now.

"I was doing a qualifying lap at Darlington and as I came out of a turn doing 185 miles an hour, I bumped the wall, my right tire blew, and I spun completely out of control."

"What happened then?" I asked, as Davis paused in his story a far away look in his eyes.

"The car flipped. Went airborne. It cleared both retaining walls and slid right into a pit crew... my own pit crew. It seriously injured my father, requiring a long hospital stay, but he recovered eventually. After that I just walked away from it all. I became a cop and here I am."

"Wow. That's some story, Lieutenant."

A few minutes of silence passed. A large toothy grin appeared on the Lieutenant's face. "Hey, I really got you didn't I?"

"You made that up?"

"I did. Believe me, I've spent more than enough time listening to stories and alibis and know how some folks can really spin a yarn. I'm sorry I had to lead you on, really I am, but stories are stories, and in my business we have to deal in facts and hard evidence. There's something we need to get to the bottom of here. My gut tells me that there will be an unusual story or explanation behind this situation, and in the end we are going to be asked to buy into it. Are you with me?"

"Yes, I am." My answer was a bit curt. I was annoyed at being led on.

Lieutenant Davis nodded at the phone on my desk. "Let's hope your many resources can untangle this mess."

For some reason I couldn't quite put my finger on, I had a sense that under the surface, a mutual respect was beginning to develop. There was more to Lieutenant Davis than there had seemed to be first. I got the idea that perhaps I was no longer just one of "the B&B people" to him. I was still a bit distracted by his phony story when I realized he was still standing.

"Come on, sit awhile. I've just been on the phone to several friends and sources in Miami, and I'm still trying to make sense of our conversations. I'm guessing you've come to interview me once more about the events of this morning, right?" Lieutenant Davis nodded.

"Well, here goes again, and I really haven't had any new thoughts since we last talked."

I proceeded to detail one more time the morning's events exactly as I remembered my movements from first hearing the splash to the arrival of the EMTs. The Lieutenant listened thoughtfully. Then he gave me the bad news.

"The coroner called me from the hospital. He refused to sign a death certificate for accidental death, or drowning. Mr. Loving, since Mr. Tydings arrived late last night, and his associates claim they didn't know he was coming here to your Bed and Breakfast, I've got a feeling one of your guests might be responsible for what appears to be the untimely death of Mr. Horace Tydings."

"Come on Lieutenant, you know how many people walk by a bed and breakfast daily. A rich show off like him would be a perfect target for a robbery of opportunity. While you're naming suspects, you might as well use the city telephone book."

The Lieutenant wiped away a line of perspiration that appeared on his brow. The man sweated like a stuffed pig. To be sure, the flannel shirt and raincoat had to be significant factors.

"You've got a point about it being anybody, but the way I figure it, the only people around here who might have known him well enough to have a beef with him are the other guests. It makes sense doesn't it?"

Shaking my head no, I reply to his theory. "In fact Lieutenant, the reservations for this weekend were quite random. They were not done as a block of four rooms. Each was done separately and on different days." I continued a bit sarcastically. "Our friend Tydings checked in late last night, not with any of the other guests, and didn't even appear for breakfast this morning. Other than the noise late last night, I doubt the other guests even knew who is in the remaining room."

"Well now, Mr. Loving, if this were some kind of random killing, you and your guests are in just as much danger as anybody else in town; but I don't believe for a second that this is random. You could suppose that we have a crazy killer on our hands who's just getting his first taste of blood. But really, I don't think anyone else is going to get killed."

"What if you're wrong, Lieutenant? What if there is someone with a real grudge against "the B&B people? This can really put a dent in business and serve as a warning to all of the bed and breakfast owners. Is there anyone you could station out here until you figure all this out?"

"I'll put a squad car across the street tonight. How's that? We'll keep our eyes and ears on this place. We'll get who's responsible, guest or not, you mark my words. But in some respects, I've got a feeling we might never find out who did this or why. The modern world is filled with random acts of violence. The only thing that surprises me is that it took so long for it to come to our little city. Events like this just don't happen here. We've had two homicides in the last two years, and confessions for both within hours."

He continued, "I guess I can tell you now that the Medical Examiner has agreed on the suspicious nature of the bruise on Tydings' face. It appears to be inconsistent with a fall into the pond. The body is now in Suite M at the hospital, waiting transfer to the State Bureau of Investigation in Garner, for autopsy."

"Wait a minute, Lieutenant. Suite M?"

"Yeah, that's the term the Emergency Room nurses use to designate the morgue. When they're talking to each other or other staff, that's what they say instead of morgue, in case any relatives or friends are near enough to overhear. It has a much nicer ring."

"Unbelievable!" Dead in the morgue really was not what I wanted to hear. "Let's go upstairs, Lieutenant, and get Chris involved in any further discussions."

"One last thing, Mr. Loving, before we leave, tell me a little about this framed discharge paper."

"Not much to tell, really. My father's family, in the mountains of New Hampshire, goes back to the early 18th Century. I found that discharge paper right after my Dad died when I was cleaning out his papers. The soldier there was my great-grandfather, and my Dad was named after him, as was my older brother. Here, you may find this interesting as well; a Pension Certificate made out to my great-grandmother Sarah for a widow's War Act pension. See, there it is, eight dollars a month, how about that! And in small print, ...she was entitled to an extra two dollars a month for each child under sixteen. The payments ended in December 1902."

Davis was genuinely impressed with this little bit of history, and explained to me his plans for the battle re-enactment.

"That sounds great. I'd appreciate it if you would let me know the details. I'd love to see it. But right now I'd like to go up to the kitchen and see how Chris is doing."

The three of us sat at the kitchen table, contemplating each other now over cups of strong tea. Lieutenant Davis continued to direct his attention toward me. Now that the history lessons were over, he became 'all cop', and tried a harsher attitude.

"Why didn't you tell me you knew Tydings from Miami? And also why didn't you tell me that you two had a strong dislike for each other."

"You didn't ask me."

"It really doesn't matter how we found out Mr. Loving, and not only do we know it now, but it appears to be pretty common knowledge, at least among business circles in Miami. Our people have been doing some checking, and it turns out that, to say the least, you two guys really didn't like each other. We were told he held you primarily responsible for costing him a lot of money in several missed opportunities."

"Your sources are pretty good Lieutenant, and I guess there is little secret about my dislike for the man."

Chris looked upset at the change in my voice. I bet she thought things may not go well from here on.

"But if I grasp your inference that this dislike extended to my doing this guy in with a rock or something on my own property and then managed to be first on the scene.......well..."

"Hold it," cried Chris, "Ed don't say something you might later regret. Just what, if anything, are you trying to say Lieutenant?"

The Lieutenant hesitated, and appeared to be struggling with a decision on what to say.

He finally declared, "Actually, nothing. I'm simply letting you in on a little of what transpired this afternoon. What I haven't told you is that we determined that Tydings companion is really a Ms. Daisy Martinez from Miami. She appears to be nothing more than just a short term squeeze for Mr. Tydings. She was extremely cooperative at the hospital and explained in graphic detail that Tydings put her up to making reservations at your lovely place for the four day holiday. According to Ms. Martinez, however, he really only intended to stay through tomorrow morning, by which time he would get his enjoyment out of having you wait on him. The plan was that on Friday they would be off to the upscale Richmond Hill Inn. Before they left though, Tydings planned to make enough of a stink about things and to humiliate you in front of the other guests and give your place a black eye, and ultimately drive you out of business.

When Ms. Martinez started spilling the beans, I sent a man over to take a statement as she talked to Sergeant Howe. "She told our Sergeant that he went crazy, he was so upset about how you acted last night. He'd done everything he could think of to make you lose your cool, and you simply treated him like you would any other tired, late arriving guest. You were polite; you were even solicitous, and totally unruffled. He wanted you to go nuts, and shout at him and wake your other guests up with your racket. When you were the polite, professional host he just about lost it. It seems he didn't believe that you had left Miami and banking on your own. He told her you were too young and egotistical to leave your career and position in the city and the banking world on your own. He was sure you were 'hiding out' here, and his arrival would make you beg him to 'keep your secret'. Ms. Martinez said he practically glowed when he said he'd have you right where you deserved to be… in his control."

After a pause and in some kind of bonded unison, Chris and I exclaimed "You're joking!"

"It's no joke. That story of her's made me get a group of my best investigators and myself on the phone checking up on you. I could hardly believe what we were all told. It is extremely rare that we get a truly consistent reading on one of our, er, not exactly suspects, but let's say 'a person of interest."

Chris looked more than indignant. I quickly put my hand on her arm to keep her from saying something she might regret. The Lieutenant noticed this.

"I'm sorry, Mrs. Loving. But you must understand, that in its initial phase, any investigation into an unexpected death has to include everyone, yes, everyone, as a possible culprit."

"Mr. Loving, this might explain my interest in your room decorations downstairs. If I had such accolades, I'd put them where everyone could see them. The message I got, loud and clear from not only your friends, but your 'rivals', or say competition, was that you were always, and they emphasized, always, professional, honest to a fault, and could coolly handle any criticism, even when totally undeserved. I can understand how you collected your plaques and letters. And while you wouldn't lend Tydings a dime, and truly despised his business practices, your background and ethics would not ever let you get into any kind of physical conflict. The expression I heard more than once was that you'd never dirty your hands or reputation by touching him."

Looking at Chris, he continued "I also learned that your wife was held in high regard too. That even though you two worked for rival banks, and could possibly sabotage the other's bank by sharing closely held information, your were both regarded too honest and loyal to do so. I was told that somehow the two of you were able to lead competing corporate lives and complementing private lives and you both were "above suspicion.""

Chris looked guardedly optimistic at the change in the Lieutenant's attitude. He now clearly was acting as the number one criminal investigation officer in our fair city. Chris saw me looking at Davis intently and certainly in a much different light. I could not realistically be considered a suspect now. Davis was actually confiding in us!

"You may enjoy this, Ed," Davis was becoming more caught up in his new found conspiratorial nature. "I also spoke with Mr. Tydings right hand man in Miami earlier this afternoon. He told me that what always got to Tydings the most was the above board way in which you dealt with him and his hired executives. Tydings was derisive, and smugly caustic in calling you, Ed, a 'dumb, honest man'. He just could not understand that; particularly in your powerful position in the bank. No, Ed, I do not see you as a prime suspect, let's face it you're not only considered to be dumb, but you're honest as well. Frankly, this really doesn't prove to be a strong enough motive."

"I guess I'll take that as a compliment. But I must tell you...'

"Hold on a minute, honey", interrupted Chris, "let's end this little meeting on its very high note! It seems a bit unrealistic that the Lieutenant will clear you right away dear, but let's not refuse it."

Lieutenant Davis nodded in agreement. "I'm telling you right now Ed everybody is going to be pushing me for a quick solution to this one. We've got an infamous businessman possibly murdered or at least a suspicious homicide according to the medical examiner. Cases like this work up a lot of public interest; everyone wants the culprit caught, and soon."

The words murdered and culprit had a chilling effect on me. No longer was there a chance Tydings death would be treated as an accident.

"Then go catch him Lieutenant!" Chris said defiantly.

"I intend to. But you know how things work; I can't give you preferential treatment yet, no matter how much I might be tempted to. I believe you're innocent, and you know you're innocent. But you sure as hell could be made to look guilty if anyone were so inclined."

I knew that. I understood it, but didn't like hearing it.

"Stay out of the investigation, Ed, spend time here at the inn, work in the yard, watch television."

I nodded in agreement, and added, "I've got an inn to run. I don't have time to play detective." But I knew that I was prepared to do just that. This was my inn, and my life and I'll be damned if I wouldn't stay involved. My back and forth down stairs on the phone would be a tip off to anyone. No way was I not going to pursue my own efforts to get to the bottom of things.

"Lieutenant, I've got to be up front with my guests, and tell them what I know is happening. At least, that way they'll have the option of leaving if they're not comfortable about staying."

"I understand that Ed. I will have to ask them to stay here in town if not here at the inn for a few days at least. I know the killer could be long gone, but I can't help feeling that he's still right here."

As he had done so often in the past, Horace Tydings had created a mess for me and once again I had to be very careful how I got myself out of it.

Lieutenant Davis was now really warming to his task, and was including Chris and me in as confederates on his investigative information.

"I personally called the headquarters of Tydings empire in Miami; basically looking for next of kin. Well, after getting transferred from this officer to that corporate officer, I finally got a call back from some 'nervous Nelly' V. P. who, get this, agreed this was a very tragic day indeed, they were trying to reach Tydings' closest relative, his son, but would rather we keep the news under wraps through tomorrow, Friday, and over the weekend until sometime Monday."

I told Davis that I was not at all surprised at this, and offered that this heartfelt loss in Miami among his closest advisors was probably being measured most importantly against concluding some bank, or merger negotiation at week's end. Also, the little bit of time tomorrow and over the weekend would give Tydings' people further time to prepare a stockholder strategy. News of Tydings death would no doubt create quite an unnecessary mess for his holdings in the market.

Davis appreciated this fast analysis and nodded in agreement. Apparently his folks had already advanced this scenario.

"At any rate," continued the Lieutenant, "I've already called the District Attorney with a heads up, and he is not eager to make any media points right now. I do expect however, that you will have some local TV activity here tomorrow, and when the victim's identity becomes known, my guess is that you can expect a good deal of national media coverage. I will try to position myself to give you whatever help and support I can with the media vultures. Remember, tourism is close to being our number one business and employer. We don't need any bad news about tourists' murders to be broadcast idly."

"Why lieutenant, I do believe you sound very much like a politician!"

"Well, Chris, my forensic people have already done their walk through, and now I have in hand a Crime Scene sketch. I'm on my way back to headquarters where I'll be meeting up with the task force personnel involved. You have to remember it's the first forty-eight hours that count. Leads are still warm, and evidence is still fresh. After that time period everything seems to cool, particularly peoples' memories of events."

A look of relief flooded Chris' face and I saw her delight at being a co-conspirator now with Lieutenant Davis. "Well one obstacle hurdled." she said.

At this point I said "It all sounds really great" as I hurried downstairs to take a call on my private line. Lieutenant Davis didn't seem to mind my taking leave at all. I heard them continue their conversation.

"You say your guests return about five o'clock, and you have a wine and cheese hour around five-thirty?"

"That's right, Lieutenant. Oops, I realize that I now have only a little time to prepare for this. In fact, I see one returning guest car in the parking lot, oh, and here comes another."

True to form, guests, regardless of their daily activities, invariably returned to the inn around five o'clock in time to freshen up for wine and cheese hour, after which they left for their dinner reservations.

"Chris, I know this may be difficult for you and Ed, but I would like to interview your guests individually tonight, and I would like a private spot to do it. Can you discuss this with Ed and make the arrangements?"

"Certainly, Lieutenant, as soon as he's off the phone."

"Chris, there's one last thing. Do you think that you and Ed could call me Richard, particularly when it's just the three of us?"

"Certainly, Richard, that would be very nice, and of course you should remember at all times we are 'Chris' and 'Ed'."

"Hey honey, were you and the Lieutenant getting along just now? I just came up for a cold drink. I have to get back to my phone calls. You look better than you have all day. Did the Lieutenant leave?"

"Well," Chris turned to me with a smile, "a major crisis behind us; now 'just' a 'nagging' problem before us. And, yes, 'Richard' as we now should call him has left only to return to quiz our guests later. I watched him from the kitchen window as he walked across the parking lot. And sure enough the first thing he did upon hitting the outside kitchen steps was to take out one of his 'little sweet buddies'; he lit up just before he got into his car and drove off. I can't imagine what the inside of that car smells like."

Unfortunately, moments later Chris' calm proved premature. From the kitchen window she recognized her least favorite local newsman emerging form his car in the parking lot. I took a couple of steps down the stairs, where I could hear them but stay out of sight. The newsman strode purposefully toward the inn and rang the back door bell.

"Hello, in there! Mr. Loving! Mr.Loving!"

"No comment!" Chris called through the window.

The reporter rolled his eyes and shook his head in frustration.

"I'm only trying to do my job here. I'd rather get a direct quote from Mr. Loving before I have to resort to using my 'sources'".

"No comment" replied Chris again.

He crossed his arms and rocked on his heels, and then his lips set in a smirk. Chris and I heard him quite well through the open window. She simply would not open the door for him.

"This must be very upsetting for you, Mrs. Loving. I'm sure you've heard the rumors that Mr. Loving is the chief suspect in Horace Tydings' untimely death earlier today. That information will be the lead story in the news."

"No comment." Chris repeated through gritted teeth. "Please leave, and tell your co-workers to stay away as well."

The thought of a possible front page article or evening news story accusing me of murder shook Chris so much that she feebly asked, "What does the article say?"

"Our sources have already informed us of the bitter hatred Mr. Tydings held for your husband, and we're told the feelings were mutual. But, hey, we'll run with it with or without your husband's response."

I watched him grin at Chris' distress, then return to his car and speed out of the parking area.

Chris was blazing mad. "Don't throw any of the crystal or the china," I told her trying to lighten the mood.

"Lieutenant Davis, oops, Richard, won't be back in his office yet. I'll tell him about this in detail later when he shows up for Wine and Cheese. After all, he did indicate that he would do his best to ward off or help with the media vultures."

I headed back downstairs to catch up with my friend and fellow innkeeper.

"I know I didn't call you before, Jerry. Things have been pretty hectic here the past few hours. I don't think I can play in the tournament; in fact I know I can't. This is so difficult for me to do to you, and I know full well how very upset you must be, Jerry."

"What do you mean you're not playing? Don't you realize the importance of us being defending champs? Everyone is expecting us to repeat. You can't miss it, I won't let you."

Jerry Holmes: best friend, golfing buddy and excellent golf tournament partner was getting worked up. This was not good for his blood pressure. "Put Ellen on the phone before you have a heart attack or something."

"You can't do this to me, uh, us, Ed. It's not fair to me, to you, to the rest of the field who expect us to defend our title of Best Ball partners from last year."

In actuality, I knew the rest of the club participants would be tickled pink to have us drop out. In his heart, Jerry knew this too.

"Calm down, Jerry, get Ellen on the phone, and I'll explain everything to you both."

Ellen Holmes was one of Chris' closest friends. The Holmes owned the beautiful *Carriage Inn*, across the street from us. They had a truly wonderful Bed and Breakfast with nine rooms, and a staff of three. It was quite an undertaking for them--- they differed from us significantly in that they had more rooms, more staff, and a large mortgage to worry about. Jerry had been a patent attorney in a large New York firm for many years until they decided to change their life style completely, and begin life anew in Asheville. We were very much alike, and thoroughly enjoyed our time together in the club events.

"Ellen? Are you on? Good, let me tell you both what happened here today." I went through the series of events one more time, not sparing a detail. "Oh, you poor guys!" was Ellen's immediate reaction.

"I did hear the EMS truck go down your street earlier, but I can't see your parking area from our front room. It's all those trees Jerry planted. I just assumed it was going someplace further on down. We did notice quite a crowd going up and down your side street. How is Chris? Maybe I can come over for a few minutes."

Ellen was being Ellen. She was the salt of the earth, a great neighbor, a great friend and a wonderful associate in the local hospitality market. Jerry was silent. I knew he now understood that this was a serious situation, and there appeared to be no way that I could just take off for a few days to play golf. I was also quite sure that Jerry's legal mind was racing around the myriad issues of liability, and unquestionably the long term effect on our reputation. Jerry, ever the pragmatist would realize and calculate the potential effect this might have on all the bed and breakfast inns in town, particularly his.

"There you have it my friends. Not a great way to start this weekend at all. Jerry you must understand that I cannot leave the inn now, nor leave Chris alone."

"Of course he does," chirped Ellen. "I heard him before, he was just being selfish and thinking about himself. The world, and even your precious golf tournament, will go on and be just fine, even without your involvement this time!"

"Thanks, Ellen. Listen; let me call you back later, along with Chris. There may be some new developments or information we can give you. In the meantime, I'm sorry to ruin your weekend, Jerry, could you please call the club, and tell them we can't make it. Please, do not repeat what I told you. Events are still a little disturbing and not quite clear. We also expect a little invasion by the local press, and I'm sure the national media at some point. So, it's going to be quite a circus over here for a while. Again, keep it under your hat and wish us good luck; speak to you later. Sorry again, Jerry."

"Oh, come on, Ed, this is serious stuff. When you first called I just didn't know what was happening. Of course I understand; and let us know if we can be of any help. Say, maybe I can get them to move the tournament to another date!"

Yes, Jerry really got it, and in doing so put my interests ahead of his own. That's what real friends did. For the first time in what seemed a long, long while I smiled.

CHAPTER IV

Wine and cheese….

Thursday 5:30 PM

I always look forward to the guests return after their day 'on the town' or in the mountains. Granted everyone is tired after a long day, yet there is always an air of optimism, and the attitude of 'let me tell you what we did'! It never ceases to amaze me that no matter how diverse the guests' activities might be they return in late afternoon within a few minutes of each other. "The cars are back" is the expression Chris and I use. The sounds of foot steps on the stairs, doors being opened and closed, activity in the butler's pantry - the silent house comes alive, and Chris and I prepare for the 'wine and cheese' period.

We are told by our guests that they look forward to wine and cheese time. Experiences of the day are shared, acquaintances are made or further cemented, and par for the course, everyone wants a piece of the innkeepers. Of course, it was exactly the same when we were the guests. We looked forward to this period at the end of the day to spend time with our hosts. The most often asked question is "What made you decide to do this?" When we traveled, we usually began with a preamble of 'We'd love to own a B&B,' or 'We've thought about doing this for years'. It was always interesting to me to hear just how people ultimately had arrived at owning a bed and breakfast. I mean, no one went to school for this. Each owner had his/her own story and explanation for pursuing this wonderful experience.

As a bed and breakfast owner myself now, I never tire of recalling aloud for our guests how Chris and I decided to drop out of corporate life and search out a complete life style change by renovating this old home and starting a bed and breakfast. The expression I most often use is 'to get repotted'. I did, however, remind people of something I had read when I was first researching the business: 'remember, it is much nicer to stay at a Bed and Breakfast than it is to own one!' Yes, our guests refer to *Newhart* when we begin discussion of our lives here at the inn.

For the wine and cheese gatherings each day, Chris takes considerable care to present her choices of cheeses in such a way as to invite ready consumption. The wine is always white, (remember: red stains the carpets,) always chilled to delicious crispness and served in Waterford crystal. Very nice! Wine is usually an excellent lubricant for conversations. All in all a very enjoyable time and guests are free to wander throughout the house, the gardens, out to the ornamental fish pond or just relax and rock on the side porch. During the winter months, most everyone thoroughly enjoys curling up in front of the fireplaces in either the large elegant living room or the cozy library.

Clearly, one of the high points of this period was the careful and tantalizing analysis of the menu basket, in order to make dinner plans. Menus were provided from a number of the restaurants that Asheville was blessed with, and which we personally recommended. Only menus from restaurants that consistently had above average food and service made it into our basket. We considered it "part of the deal" for our guests to end their wonderful day with a memorable dining experience. However, we always mentioned that like every other town in the USA, Asheville had what is called a 'strip' along Tunnel Road in east Asheville that had every fast food franchise known to Western man. When the guests decided where to eat, we insisted upon calling to make the reservations for them, as we felt this introduction by us gave our guests the best possible chance for a wonderful dining experience at the restaurant. Always, the little extra. If anyone returned from dinner with a complaint, Chris or I made sure the owner was quietly informed of the disappointment. The owners were surprisingly grateful for the feedback. This part of the business makes it necessary for us to eat out at the local restaurants fairly often to ensure that the quality is continuing, so most of the owners and certainly the reservation people knew us by name and by sight and often by voice on the telephone. We called this 'Research and Development', and certainly a true business expense....... a 'tough job', but someone had to do it. Our experience was even more enjoyable when the owner picked up the tab.

So it was that at the tail end of this very disturbing day, our guests were fortunately brimming with enthusiasm, anxious to talk about their activities, and simply comfortable in enjoying *Polite Society*. Two of the couples were from Florida, the Oates and the Kerrys. They arrived around eight o'clock last night, well after the wine and cheese period. The other younger couple, John and Sherry Greenlee, from Greensboro who had checked in yesterday afternoon and were here alone during yesterdays wine and cheese, now seemed to be quite happy with the larger group.

In spite of everything good, conversation couldn't help but turn immediately to the yellow crime scene tape around the koi pond and in the rear gardens.

Chris and I were prepared for this and had discussed it prior to everyone coming down. We decided that the best tack to take would be a clear and concise recitation of the facts, and let them know that shortly a Lieutenant Davis would be here to interview each of them individually. This was just a normal procedure in the case of a sudden death.

We explained that first and foremost we were most anxious that every one feel comfortable enough to stay for the complete weekend. This was the major weekend of the year, with a series of interesting and fun events from Thursday through Sunday. This of course accounted for the check-ins on Wednesday night. It was our considered opinion that Horace Tydings' accident was a thoroughly isolated incident. We also made it clear that we would certainly understand if anyone wanted to cancel the remainder of their stay here, though they might find it difficult to find accommodations within the city.

It was, after all, Bele Chere weekend!

Asheville and Western North Carolina were home to many unique and diverse 'happenings', but nothing brings such a collaboration of activities as Bele Chere. The name was often misspelled, but never mistaken for anything less than our city's most comprehensive, eclectic route to midsummer enjoyment.

The organizing committee estimated that over 550,000 people would attend this year's festival, and enjoy the wide variety of art, music, food and demonstrations that make Bele Chere the largest free outdoor festival in the southeast.

Of course my particular passion was funnel cakes and sausage and onions Po Boys, the smoke and aroma of which just seems to call my name. It truly was a great weekend and we usually hyped the guests enough for them to enjoy the lesser advertised activities such as ice carving demonstrations, juggling and street performers, and didn't forget a local favorite: clogging demonstrations.

At one of our Chamber of Commerce meetings I was given a poster from the inaugural event in 1979. The wording at that time was "Bele Chere is crepes, costumes and clogging. Bele Chere is bluegrass, weaving, crafts, parades and photography." The list goes on and on closing with "Bele Chere is downtown Asheville".

This year's poster simply showed a sumptuous tide of color tumbling over a lively musical street scene. "Bele Chere is downtown Asheville, it sings."

Enough said. All I wanted to say was: "bring on the funnel cakes."

The guests were all downstairs from freshening up in their rooms, each with a glass of wine and casually gathered in the parlor. It was now time to explain the crime scene outside, and Lieutenant Davis' interview process.

My description of the events was short and sweet, and surprisingly brought few expressions of sympathy. The kind of reaction quite frankly, I would have expected from people who actually knew HoraceTydings. To my knowledge, no one had met Tydings because of his very late check-in and the fact that he did not come down for breakfast this morning. So, in a way, no one could really personalize this tragic event. All in all, it actually went far smoother that I would have imagined, with most concerns raised over the required police interviews.

The youngest couple, John and Sherry Greenlee, was resolute in their desire to stay the weekend. This was a get-away they had planned for some time and had gone to great efforts to arrange time off at their respective employers. They also had some non refundable deposits out there on certain Bele Chere events. Horace Tydings appeared to mean nothing to them, and while they murmured the requisite sympathetic comments they remained determined to have a great weekend, regardless.

"I hope we can get this interview over with early, Ed, Sherry and I would like to make early dinner reservations. We have a full day tomorrow, and we want to get a good night's sleep."

Youth! Here we have a terrible and suspicious accident in the rear gardens, the police are interested in individually interviewing all guests and these kids think of eating and a good night's sleep. That's what makes horse races!

Bill and Mary Oates from Gainesville, Florida, when asked, were of a similar mind, to stay through the weekend. They explained that this was their fifteenth wedding anniversary, and her sister was baby sitting their thirteen year old twins. This was their first chance to get away alone in a few years. Bill Oates did know of Horace Tydings, in fact he had lost his job as Chief Financial Officer at a company Tydings had purchased. Small world, I thought, but Oates, at least on the surface seemed sincere in his feeling that this was truly a shame, Tydings reputation, not-withstanding. The last couple, John and Barbara Kerry from Orlando, Florida, was a lot less talkative than they had been at breakfast. A little strange I thought. I found them on the porch by themselves. Barbara was a little more animated than her husband and indicated her parents had provided them a Gift Certificate to *Polite Society* for the entire stay, which she and John could not afford otherwise, and they definitely were staying through Sunday. John was a nice kid but wasn't particularly interested in talking about Tydings, and appeared to be the most anxious concerning the police interview.

"Do you think it will take long?" John asked. "We really have nothing to offer the police. We weren't here all day. What could they ever want with us? Just a little harassment I suppose. Apparently they have no one else to intimidate. Like we came all the way here to Asheville to murder this guy."

I was a little taken aback by this outburst which seemed totally out of character, and really uncalled for. John was certainly on edge for some reason, and come to think of it, who had ever mentioned murder? I wanted to leave the Kerry couple alone for awhile. I was glad we were on the porch, and no one else heard this exchange. The kid had put his finger on it though. It was murder, pure and simple.

Inside, in the parlor, individual conversations on other topics, by means of Chris's clever guidance were developing rapidly. The mood had lifted, wine glasses were refilled and the basket of menus was presented. Now we were getting down to the important things --- a lively discussion of the local restaurants!

Additional talk turned to the usual questions about the inn - the wonderful furniture and other furnishings "right out of our house in New York, by way of Miami" we said. We raised four kids with most of this furniture. No one ever seemed to believe this, but it was true. The overall effect in the parlor is set by a rich deep Williamsburg Market Square Green paint, set off with softly glowing cream colored chair rails, floor moldings and wonderfully ornate crown moldings. The wood of the furniture pieces was deep cherry or mahogany and generally still bearing the scent of an aggressive wax polish. The wing chairs and camel back sofa were done in beautiful yellow brocade. We had purchased these pieces twenty-five years earlier and could hardly have guessed how appropriate the fabric of twining dogwood branches and blossoms would be in North Carolina, where the dogwoods bring such wonderful brightness to the spring forests, and is the state flower. Complimenting the Williamsburg motif are strong oriental touches, particularly a pair of antique foo dogs gracing the ends of the antique cabinet that housed our state of the art music system. When in use, the flames from the fireplace would send flashes of light dancing off the lovely crystal, beautiful porcelains and ceramics scattered throughout the room. ...And always the question: "Aren't you afraid of breakage or theft of these items?" "Not really. The bed and breakfast industry journals invariably tell us that theft is not a major industry concern. The profile of bed and breakfast guests is one of basically honest travelers who are quite simply more interested in enjoying pieces of art than in stealing them, and are usually very careful if they chose to handle a piece for a closer look."

John and Barbara Kerry came in from the porch to join us. He still didn't look very happy to me and Barbara appeared upset. Damn that Tydings, even in his absence he was ruining this weekend for some.

Overall, I was pleased with how the guests had gotten through our explanation of what occurred, and now were back feeling pretty excited about the weekend. I set out another chilled carafe of wine. In doing so I had a strong feeling that there was no way any of our guests could have been involved in this. I fully understood that this was a serious matter.

But quite selfishly, I couldn't help worrying about how this would be looked upon by the neighborhood, the Chamber of Commerce, the other bed and breakfasts in town, and God forbid!, the travel writers and tourism publications.

I needed a quiet minute away to think about things while Chris continued to engage the guests. There was a lot of damage control to think about. It called for Chris and me to sit down, and go through a select list of people to call --- we needed to put the very best spin on this! We couldn't let people create their own story. The good Lieutenant arrived and broke the spell as I sat thinking and puffing on my cigar on the kitchen steps.

"Hey, Ed, is this a good time? As I explained earlier to Chris, what I'd like to do is sit down with each guest. An initial interview we call it, nothing intimidating about the process at all. I'll want just a short explanation of their activities from say after breakfast until ten o'clock this morning."

"We've already spoken to them, Lieutenant. They seem pretty cool about it all, and I don't think you'll have any trouble getting them to make statements. You can use the dining room for a good bit of privacy. Let me go inside and round them up for you. Ha! Sounds like a movie line - 'round up the usual suspects'."

Lieutenant Davis appeared to struggle for even a weak smile.

Okay, this was good, I thought. Suspicion was off me, and I was sure that pretty soon it would be off our guests as well. Any further investigation would probably concentrate on the victim, and because of what he was, I guessed the world at large. It was a certainty that Tydings was not a beloved individual anywhere.

"It's getting late, let me start bringing them in, and I'll make their dinner reservations according to the order you chat with them. Anything else?"

"No, that's fine Ed. I'm ready for the first guest."

During the day, the Tydings room had been very quietly, and without any fan fare, cleared out of all personal belongings. The police had been quite efficient in this regard. The forensic folks had been through the room earlier in the day, perhaps on the off chance some item of evidence might appear. At this point the room was empty, and I must admit that I was thinking, albeit a bit morbidly, that we had an available room for the remainder of the weekend. I'd mention the available room to Ellen and Jerry later, when we filled them in on what was happening. Their inn always had an overflow they couldn't accommodate. I knew that Daisy Martinez would not be back. She was being held as a material witness until her story checked out. After her remarks to Sergeant Howe I knew she wouldn't be back to this 'old house full of old stuff.'

Over the next hour, Lieutenant Davis was true to his word. He met with everyone, got their initial statements, and explained that if he needed anything else it would be done tomorrow.

The guest couples were either waiting for each other or already off to dinner as their little chats with Lieutenant Davis progressed. I noticed several messages had backed up in the answering machine, and told Chris I would take them downstairs in my office.

Dinner reservations had been made as requested and now all the guests were out to dinner. Lieutenant Davis joined us in the kitchen.

"You know, Ed, the guests all have what seem to be really good alibis. You and Chris vouch for the fact that no guest had a car in the parking area or was on the property when you discovered the body in the pond. That seems to exonerate your guests. You would have seen or heard a car in the parking area when you came running back."

"That's right, that's what we said!" Chris had a touch of exasperation in her voice. We three were alone in the house now, comparing notes.

"I don't know about you Lieutenant, but I talked to all the guests, and it seemed very clear to me that none of them except Tydings and Ms. Martinez were here when I heard the splash. I had seen the three couples off after breakfast, and I hadn't heard any return. The Tydings limo had not come back either.

"I know, Ed, I got the same story."

"Are you going to restrict their movements and make them stay in town?" asked Chris.

"No, they're free to go where they please, we have good IDs, and we have legitimate home addresses. I will want an immediate call if someone packs up and wants to leave unexpectedly. You've been watching too many detective stories, Chris", the Lieutenant quipped. "And, that leads me to another point, and I want your full cooperation on this. I do not want you two acting as amateur detectives. I want you both to go about your business, and leave the investigative and detective work to the professionals. Can I get your agreement on that?"

Chris and I looked at each other and nodded in accord.

"Good! You know this is officially a homicide, folks. This is serious business. Oh, I've had the crime scene tape removed from your back yard, so for all intents and purposes, what happened here today should be transparent to your neighbors by the morning. I told the guests not to talk to anyone, and I know our people know the value of keeping everything in confidence. So, I hope you do not spread the word so to speak, even if you feel you need an effective spin for the sake of your business. Again, please, give us the next forty-eight hours to ferret out any leads we have, before you go public. Also refer any local media questions to me. We have stock answers for EMS accidents. Can I count on you?"

Davis knew something, or thought he knew something. "Ed, again, please leave the investigation of this crime to us. I promise to share with you all I can as information is developed."

"Sure, Lieutenant, uh, Richard, you can count on us." Lieutenant Davis was out the back door now. Like clock work he lit up one of his sickeningly sweet little cigars as soon as he reached the bottom step. As he walked across the parking lot he stopped a few times, looking like he had something to say and wanted to return. The good Lieutenant reached his car, and before getting in looked around at the inn one last time. He seemed to have made up his mind, got settled behind the wheel, and drove off into the night.

"Well, honey, lets close up and go across!" 'Going across' was our shorthand for walking along the slate path through the rose and herb garden to our private cottage. We were quite resolute about our living conditions when the subject of old houses and renovations started. We were adamant about having a neat, modern and comfortable place to live. No basement quarters for us. And it had to be removed from the main house. So, we renovated and enlarged the garage and this is where we now sought refuge. I would often joke that it was the best commute to work I ever had - forty feet!

Our lovely sitting room was surrounded on three sides with airy windows and louvered shutters. The bay window where Felicia, our cat, liked to sun herself and watch the birds faced the back of the inn so we could see the guests return to the inn by way of the library steps in the back. Very few guests bothered to take the pathway all the way around the house to the front door when returning at night, although they almost always took the stroll along the path to the front gardens when coming and going in the daylight. Our little cottage also offered a full, if tiny, kitchen, a good sized bedroom with wonderful closet space and a large bathroom with a Jacuzzi tub and separate shower. It was a wonderful concept and the envy of all the other innkeepers in town who were either relegated to basement quarters or God forbid- the attic!

The cottage sat right in the middle of the rear gardens and looked out on the koi pond. A wonderful sight indeed, on every day but today.

As usual, we left the house lighted for the guests' return, and to make an attractive show from the front and side streets. Chris could never understand why some innkeepers turned the lights down when the guests left for dinner. A brightly lighted house was such a welcoming sight, and probably added as much to repeat business as her ever present cookies and brownies, and seasonal drinks in the butler's pantry. But tonight the doors would be locked. The guests had their own keys.

What a day, I thought, as I walked the flagstone path to the cottage.

"Chris, you settle down with a cup of tea and let me wander around a little while outside and have a much needed *good* cigar. We'll call Ellen and Jerry when I get back."

I was proud of my inventory of cigars, which could meet my particular needs of the moment. I had some Key West "Havana wannabes" in the humidor, along with some Monte Cristo cigars from my son Everett's in-laws in Canada. Everett had his own thriving accounting and financial services firm near Ottawa. He'd married a Canadian, Dawn, a young woman with three daughters, giving him an instant family to go with his only child, a son. Fortunately his wife was also an accountant, and a real presence in the Canadian General Accountants organization. Although her office was in Ottawa, she handled standards and ethics for members all across Canada. Everett's in-laws in Thunder Bay made at least one trip annually to Havana, and did not come back empty handed. I also had an assortment of lesser priced and unknown cigars for golf and gardening. I grabbed a Monte Cristo from the humidor and went outside to smoke and ponder.

I loved the property at night almost as much as during the day. The neighborhood was quiet, except for the summer song of the cicadas, which over time had become no more than background noise I barely noticed. The shadows of the large stone inn cast by the streetlamps were comforting and familiar. Tonight, however, I did feel a little uneasy, a chill, as I passed by the pond. Just a few hours earlier had someone been murdered here? It was eerie and not very comfortable to be sure.

I must admit to wasting little time in the rear, and walked very quickly around to the front gardens.

There was no way that I could stand by and do nothing about this murder. This was my property, my business, and for the time being, my whole future. My name, my reputation and the good standing of the inn were at stake here. I had a lot to think about. Someone had deliberately despoiled my inn. It seemed a guest of our inn had been murdered and the one responsible was still on the loose. Why? There was nothing stolen. Was it Tydings himself, or was he simply in the wrong place at the wrong time? How could this lovely inn be the wrong place? Was it over? Would there be more? God, what a sorry thought. And here I was wandering around alone in the dark. I really should have had more sense.

My thoughts were pretty much jumbled up now, but one thing was very clear; this inn which was our idyllic world, had been tragically interrupted and I'd be damned if I were going to stand idly by. As much as I would like to dismiss it, I could not help thinking that one of our guests might hold the answer to my questions. No one goes off to a Bed and Breakfast to kill someone ….do they? Nonsense.

It was now getting late, close to 11 PM, I'd been out here for some time. All the guests had come back, couple by couple, and let themselves in for the night. It was time to go in and close up for the night, then go sit with Chris. Whew, what a day!

CHAPTER V

The innkeepers....

Thursday 11:30 PM

"I locked up, and took care of the lights."

"Good," replied Chris who was already in bed trying to concentrate on her current novel. "I'm not sleepy; I just can't stop thinking about all that happened today."

I nodded. "I know what you mean. I'm tired too but far from being sleepy. I'm really kind of wired! Oh, I forgot! We were supposed to call Ellen and Jerry. We'll have to do that in the morning."

Chris put her book aside and sat straight up. "Ed, honey, I have something to discuss with you. And while you may get a little upset right now, everything is to be cleared up tomorrow morning. Promise me you'll listen to me carefully, and please hear me out until I finish! Promise?"

I could see she was quite serious, and in keeping with the rest of the drama today, I replied "Of course I will listen to you and be guided by your advice."

"All right mister, just sit down and listen. In tomorrow's *Citizen Times* there will be a story about Horace Tydings and you and your relationship in Miami. The upshot is it's probably a very one sided story about your dislike for him and his taunting and badgering you, which no doubt will provide the idea that you are a prime suspect in his untimely death. I suppose the idea was to put you on trial via the press and the court of public opinion over the next few days. We both know the paper's mission in life is to sell newspapers, so let's not give it any more meaning than that. I discussed this with Lieutenant Davis tonight, and he's going to arrange to be interviewed and quoted for the news sometime tomorrow. Listen to me; you are not, according to the Asheville police and the District Attorney, to be considered the prime suspect in the death of Horace Tydings. Lieutenant Davis will make sure the local TV and the newspapers quote him as saying that this is just the story of an unfortunate accident. Lieutenant Davis wants the person actually responsible to believe that he has gotten away with murder. Then he might get careless, and they'd have a better chance of catching him.

Chris looked hopefully at me. "Well, can you go with this for one day, regardless of the story tomorrow?"

"I'm cool! I'm not going to get excited! You've covered the situation. This just confirms my low opinion of the local newspaper. Lieutenant Davis appears to be a man of his word, and quite honestly, having a rather direct statement such as he intends, is the best thing that could happen. It takes any question of my involvement away, and hopefully will embarrass the newspaper. I see it as win-win."

I thought to myself that this only fortified my intention of seeking out the real killer. Chris didn't have to know of my intention to get more involved in the solution.

"Oh, Ed, thank you. You're being as calm and wonderful as usual."

Not for the first time did Chris pinch herself about being lucky enough to spend her life with me. I was her man and her hero.

I had been a very successful banker. I started out years ago on the Executive Training Program of a large money center bank in New York City, right after my required military service and obtaining my MBA from NYU. This military duty had involved two years in Frankfurt, Germany, in Military Intelligence, which Chris was quite fond of terming an 'oxymoron'. She was convinced of this after hearing the tales of my rather juvenile exploits with my buddies at the various Officers Clubs and local bars in Europe, to say nothing of what went on at the Oktoberfest celebrations in Germany. She swore that tales of my exploits were, by all accounts, hardly military, and certainly were not very intelligent. Chris would chuckle agreeably when I would tell folks that, in all good conscience, perhaps I should have paid the government rather than drawing my pay while on duty in Germany. Both of our remarks about this period of my life were normally tongue in cheek and good for a few laughs. In my defense I did insist, quite rightly, that all was calm throughout the world during my tour of duty and nothing untoward happened "during my watch."

I had done well at my original bank, but left at the age of twenty-nine for the unusual opportunity of becoming President of a small independent bank in Queens, New York. That bank had been a correspondent client of my original bank, and the difficult and demanding owner of it had asked my superiors for a chance to speak to one of their brightest stars. This led to my tenure as the youngest bank president in New York history. There were few more calculated moves prior to arriving in Miami to assume the leadership of the corporate activities of Barnett Bank, which ultimately became Florida's largest bank. Over the years I grew in stature as did Barnett. I sat on many civic, charitable and educational boards, and was deemed "a player" in Miami circles. I was particularly proud of one accolade from the President of a rival bank who, upon my departure for Asheville, claimed: "You certainly made a difference!"

Now I was just another small businessman. I may have traded my Brooks Brothers' suits and Gucci loafers for LL Bean duds, but my ego remained fully intact – and large. At fifty-five years old I was in relatively good shape. I was active, well tanned from hours on the fairways, slightly gray, and still a very handsome man. My blue eyes had long lashes that Chris described as lady-killers. I walked with purpose, with that bounce in my step familiar to athletes. I was particularly proud to have been inducted into the Citadel Athletic Hall of Fame. My baseball exploits at school were certainly in the past, but still remained very cherished and proud memories. I spoke with quiet authority and had a very pleasant way of meeting folks on whatever level they desired.

Chris just wished I would get rid of my damn cigars! I could also use some diplomacy pills for dealing with the media.

Inn keeping was now my chosen life. There was no detail, large or small, about the business or property that I was not aware of, and didn't have an opinion about. I loved every aspect of it!

"What are you smiling at? What are you thinking?" I asked Chris. She had that silly little warm smile that I liked so much. She actually looked at peace. She was the best. I was so lucky to have found the perfect compliment and perfect partner, even if I had to admit that all of our kids liked her best. She was the first one they turned to when in need of any kind of assistance.

I swore that there was no way I wouldn't try to get to the bottom of this. I won't discuss what I'm doing with Chris yet, but I've already reached out to some folks in Miami about Tydings latest deals, and others will call back tomorrow.

I knew it was best to hold off telling Chris until something concrete was developed. She, on the other hand, bless her heart, will play it by the book with Lieutenant Davis. Huh, even in my mind I can't get comfortable calling him Richard, yet. Maybe when this was all over, and he was no longer "the police" and I wasn't a question mark in some people's minds, I'd find it easier to accept him on a first name person. Chris told him that she wouldn't get involved, and there is no question that she would be true to her word.

Chris went back to her reading; now completely absorbed. As always I knew how lucky I was to have Chris as my partner, my lover, and as the kids say, my soul mate. She was so darn smart too! If I were that smart I would be king, no kidding. She had very comfortably assumed the role of family matriarch when my mother passed away. At the beginning this was assumed to be an impossible task by most family members. But Chris prevailed. I looked over at her with much affection. I thought back. The idea of dropping out of our corporate careers in Miami to pursue a 'lifestyle change' in Asheville had been mine and mine alone. When traveling we had stayed in bed and breakfasts for the most part, and the ambience always appealed to me. It seemed such a gracious and unhurried way of life. Often when we would find ourselves curled up on a comfortable porch, or in front of a cozy fireplace with a good supply of paperback books, I would casually remark to Chris, "You know, we could do this." Well, this latent desire went on for several years until I finally got frustrated enough at the bank. I was "a dinosaur – at fifty years old!" But that's what happened.

At the bank I turned around one day and everyone else seemed to be less than thirty years old, and was using computers to make decisions. They had no sense of, or appreciation for history, character, or community benefit, and to my way of thinking, not likely to develop any. Chris, bless her heart, was an all-star at her institution, a rival bank.

She was extremely competent, well liked and very happy in her job. She liked Miami, too, which for me had become too crowded, too dangerous and truly had become the "best city in Latin America"! But Chris agreed to our move to Asheville, had left behind the job, the position she loved so much, and the management and employees who valued her talents and leadership. As I expected, she was tireless in getting the business going; an integral part of everything we had accomplished. When my mother was alive she often told me how lucky I was to find Chris. And I believed her. Of course in my absence she told Chris how lucky she was to find me. My mother was a very savvy lady. We both missed her terribly. There was a picture of Florence on one of the tables in the parlor, and we talked to her as we passed. We asked her, quite often "How are we doing?" During her lifetime, she would never hesitate to answer this question. Chris was another formidable woman, attractive, stately, intelligent and conscientious; an opinion I always knew that I shared with her former bosses.

Now in the final analysis we had to face facts. A guest had been murdered in our backyard. "Why?" was the most compelling question. Would there be someone else? Was it only to be Tydings? Was someone after me, or was it a random bit of violence? Hell, somehow it might have been a highly unusual, yet tragic accident. I wouldn't hold my breath on that one. But, this whole series of what ifs was scary. I constantly revisited in my mind those 10 or 15 seconds that it took to get to the pond after hearing the splash. How did someone leave the property so quickly? Why didn't I see anyone leaving the property, or even hear a car leaving? I knew Chris was having similar thoughts. I got angry just thinking about this. Someone had invaded my space, and sure as hell made a mess of things; but I had to be calm! Yeah, I was calm! I couldn't even repeat a story for Lieutenant Davis that I didn't get testy and a little confrontational. Okay, Chris was already asleep, tomorrow is another day, we still have guests, and breakfast was expected to be a memorable time at *Polite Society*---just like our advertising said.

At that, Chris rolled over, and stirred awake. She noticed me still awake, playing with my glasses --- "That's enough Sherlock, turn off the light, get some sleep and let the police catch our murderer". She was really good! How did she know?

Early the next morning before the sun had a chance to rise I rushed outside and grabbed the newspaper. I unfolded the paper, held my breath and opened it to the front page. There it was. A file photograph, a studio portrait, taken of me for the Board of Trustees of Barry University accompanied the headline that read: <u>B&B OWNER'S HIDDEN PAST.</u> I gave the article a quick scan to assess the damage. It was in fact shorter than I had envisioned. The opening paragraph was slanted to catch the readers' attention:

"Confirmed sources have revealed that Ed Loving, owner of *Polite Society*, a local Bed and Breakfast was a bitter business enemy of Horace Tydings, a Miami, FL business tycoon, who was found dead under mysterious circumstances yesterday morning at Mr. Loving's Inn. Mr. Tydings was a registered guest. According to sources, the two had acrimonious business relations to the point of it being a long term grudge, and anonymous sources indicate that Mr. Loving looms as a prime suspect."

In a particularly shoddy performance, the reporter had not interviewed the police to get their reactions, and only a one sentence mention was made that Mr. Loving could not be reached for comment. From this the giant leap to 'prime murder suspect' had been made. Alright they didn't spell out 'murder' but every reader would see the word there. Except for the splashy headline, it was pretty much an example of the newspaper's unerring ability to be grossly misleading and most often inaccurate. If that's all there would be, this might not be too serious a problem to counter, especially if the TV picked up the Lieutenant's new conference early in the day. I tucked the paper tightly under my arm and went back to the cottage.

Chris and I proceeded on auto pilot through waking, showering and dressing for the day. A work day, if you will. There were the usual early morning duties and rituals that must be done in order to have breakfast served promptly at 8:30 AM.

Make the coffee and deliver a carafe of coffee and cups to the upstairs hallway! A wonderful touch, and always appreciated by the guests, both the serious coffee drinkers or just someone pleased by yet another thoughtful detail. A lot of guests liked the first cup of coffee in the privacy of their room, as they dressed. Set the table, open the doors, turn on the breakfast music, and hide this morning's local paper. That's it, we have guests, and everything must appear normal. In some ways yesterday seemed like a hundred years ago, the tranquility and peace and beauty of the old inn were asserting themselves again. It was like nothing had happened.... but it had. I won't insult these people now; if someone wants to talk about it we will, if not, we won't ---- their call!

My usual schedule was to finish up around 8 AM and sit on the side porch with a cup of coffee and a cigar until around 8:25 when I went back in to welcome the guests as they came downstairs. I know the cigar annoyed Chris, because she always explained that it made me smell like smoke, and might offend a guest as I placed their breakfast entrée plate in front of them with a practiced flourish. As usual she was right, but I always maintained that my charming and captivating personality usually carried the day. Cool man! I was sure I could pull it off this morning.

What I keep thinking was: if I were going to catch a murderer, where do I start? How do I do this?

The Greenlees came down first.

"Good morning to you, John and Sherry. Sleep well?"

"Like a log, Ed", responded John, "but you know, all we could think about over dinner last night was the terrible accident. We know too, that with the Lieutenant coming to ask everyone where they were during the morning, that he thinks there is more to this than an accident. Does he believe it was a homicide?"

I really did not want to hear this.

John gave Sherry a glance. "You know this is really kind of disconcerting. Do you think we're safe here? Was it random? Can we do anything?"

I jumped in, "John this is business for the police to deal with. In any unexpected death they have to look at all the possibilities until they are satisfied with the original appearance of an accident. We're here to make your stay enjoyable. The exciting Bele Chere weekend events will go on. Please try to dismiss these thoughts while you're here."

"Oh, I know we will," replied Sherry, with a little twinkle in her eye, "but you know, it's a little like those mystery weekends some Bed and Breakfasts put on. You wouldn't do that to us as a surprise, would you?"

"Sherry, I assure you that yesterday was the real deal. This is not a charade. But, please, I urge you to put it out of your mind and make the most of your remaining weekend here in Asheville."

On the spur of the moment, and to counter any further speculation, I quickly said "Chris and I would like to give you and the other couples a gift certificate for a future complimentary weekend. It seemed the least we can do for the inconvenience of last night with Lieutenant Davis, and perhaps the uncertainty of everything."

"Oh, Ed, that's great," said Sherry as she punched John in the arm. "When are we coming next John? Now we can afford it again with the gift certificate."

John looked a little sheepish. "Thanks Ed. Sherry and I will definitely plan on coming back for another weekend, maybe in October. I understand the leaf changes are beautiful."

"They are," I replied. Oh dear, I thought, the best time of the year, 100% occupancy if you want it, a cash flow dream, the time of the year that most Bed and Breakfasts get financially healthy. Wouldn't you know, here I was supplying gift certificates for this overbooked time. I really should have thought this through. I couldn't help thinking that trying to be a Sherlock Holmes is getting in the way of running the inn properly. Chris will just have to go along with this.

This mental slip reminded me of certain ground rules we had set up at the inception of the business. First: if I or Chris made a mistake, it was not to be dwelled upon, but to be learned from and we'd move on wiser, if not happier. Second: If we were to have a 'meeting', it would last no more than a couple of minutes, and would conclude with a clear decision. I knew that in both cases the rules were the product of our often frustrated large corporate existences. I heard the other couples on the landing.

"Come on everyone, let's go in and have breakfast!"

As I said before, it was highlighted in our brochures, and included in all print advertising, "Breakfast is a memorable time at *Polite Society*. Fine china, Waterford crystal, sterling silver service"--- just like home, huh?

With everyone together, the interaction of the guests was an important ingredient in the whole Bed and Breakfast experience. Naturally I served and responded quite well to compliments on the service and was not above pandering on this score. I am also quite adept, when conversation might be flagging, to stimulate the table with some anecdote, or perhaps the introduction of a controversial topic sure to get people talking. The latest celebrity criminal, ACC basketball, women at The Citadel, (my alma mater), were just a few of tried and true ice breakers.

"Say, what's the latest on the investigation, Ed?" called out Bill Oates. "That Lieutenant Davis was really a pretty good guy last night in his interviewing. He didn't overpower us with questions, and I must say he was more than polite. Does he know what he's doing? I mean to hear him; this is a suspicious accident- could be a homicide for heaven's sake. Some of us were wondering if we were really okay here. I don't want to ruin breakfast, but what do you think Ed?"

"I say, who needs another cup of coffee? Hazelnut coffee at its best!" There was no way this guy was going to ruin Chris' Stuffed French Toast. The stuffing was cream cheese, crushed pineapple and pecans, with a lovely apricot sauce. She made her own bread for this treat; double apricot almond bread. Whooee!

I continued. "We had a long chat with the lieutenant yesterday, and he never mentioned a mad killer on the loose, or an unsafe situation at *Polite Society*. From this it's my opinion it was an isolated incident, and Horace Tydings brought his own troubles with him."

John and Sherry Greenlee were deeply involved in savoring the French toast. Bill Oates now had a bemused expression on his face, and the Kerrys, well Barbara looked a little pensive, and into herself, while Phil was mumbling something about random violence, and looked surprisingly uncomfortable. That seemed to be the end of it; talk shifted to anticipated activities for the day, the Biltmore House, and suggested parking plans during the day. The city was so crowded with visitors and it put unusual strains on parking and our limited mass transit system. We knew where the special park and ride lots were set up for this weekend, and had maps ready for our guests.

The French toast disappeared nicely, as it always did, and everyone was a member, at least for this morning, of the clean plate club.

On the way upstairs Bill and Mary Oates stuck their heads in the slightly ajar kitchen door. "Chris, breakfast was great, again. Of course the service was impeccable," said Mary. This was my cue to bow, as

I generally play up to the guests for such not so unsolicited remarks. Ha!

Bill continued, "Oh, Ed, please forgive my remarks in the dining room before, my shins are still stinging from Mary's kicks under the table. I didn't mean to put you on the spot, I don't know, just doing some thinking out loud, I guess. We're very happy to be here, we're enjoying our room, the ambiance of the house, certainly the food, and of course the inn-keepers. We'll try not to give yesterday's accident another thought. But, hey, listen Ed, between you and me, and the lamp post, and not for Lieutenant Davis' ears, I can't think of a more deserving person for an accident such as this, than Horace Tydings."

"William," commanded Mary Oates from several steps ahead on the stairs, "you hush up. Thanks again, Chris, Ed."

Bill Oates closed the door and they were on their way.

"See there's another fan of Tydings. This really seems beyond coincidence, but what do I know." I gave Chris the shoulder shrug.

I was so worried yesterday about the guest's reaction and now this. These people appear a cool lot; a little wine, a good meal, Chris's French toast, the Biltmore House, Bele Chere; they all have more important things to think about than a body in the back garden's pond.

I turned to Chris who was hand washing my mother's gold embossed wedding china. "So what do we do today? You know, it's almost twenty-four hours exactly from the time of the big splash yesterday. I'm trying to change my schedule, do things a little differently."

"I think you're a little paranoid, myself," chirped Chris. She went on, "My instincts tell me that this was indeed an isolated incident, probably an accident to start with, but no less a tragic and serious incident at this point. Those are my thoughts Ed, and as far as I'm concerned, we can go on about our daily business, and put this entire episode behind us."

Whew, anyone else and I would pooh-pooh the idea, but Chris? She grinned, "Don't you agree with me. Mr. Innkeeper, man for all seasons, love of my life?"

"Does this mean I can play in the tournament this weekend?" I ducked just in time as a small piece of apricot bread came whizzing by my ear. "Hey!"

"Oh, oh, we didn't call Ellen and Jerry last night. Let me get them on the line, and you can fill them in and get their professional analysis." Another piece of bread came flying at me. "Hey!" I repeated.

Ellen Holmes answered on the first ring, "The Carriage Inn, this is Ellen, how may I help you."

I couldn't help but reflect that these gals were so good at this. Jerry was indeed lucky to have such a good and friendly partner. He would not survive without Ellen. Come to think of it, maybe I wouldn't either, without Chris.

"Ellen, Ed here, let me put Chris on the line; she'll bring you up to speed. We're really not supposed to be talking about this to anyone, Lieutenant Davis's orders."

"Come on, Ed," countered Ellen, "you wouldn't hold out on us would you? I certainly hope not. I'm sorry to hear that you shouldn't talk to us about it. Now, please stay cool, Ed, and tell us about the front page article in today's paper. Also, I think your friend and mine, Jerry, told the Pro at the Club what happened when he cancelled for the tournament."

"That's great Ellen; I can see him holding court in the men's card room at the club!" Lieutenant Davis was sure to think I was out gabbing.

"Ellen, here's Chris!" With my hand over the receiver I proclaimed to Chris, "you might as well tell Ellen what you want, that jerk Jerry is up at the club gabbing his head off. Here, I'm going downstairs to return a few calls.

"Hi, Ellen," said Chris gaily, giving me a good wink, "I bet we had more excitement at our inn yesterday than you had at yours!"

I stomped out of the kitchen thinking everyone around me had gone mad!

CHAPTER VI

The media....

Friday, mid-day

I was in my office when the call came mid-morning from a production assistant at Channel 13, our local TV station.

"Mr. Loving I understand you've had quite a gruesome murder at your B&B. We'd like to send some one by, along with a camera man, to interview you for more details."

"Hello ... hello ..., we must have a bad connection, I can't hear you." I proceeded to hang up. This happened one more time with the same result.

After making a call to Lieutenant Davis I went back upstairs, and told Chris of the media calls.

"We should have expected this I guess." Chris had completed her morning briefing of Ellen and paused to give me some calming words.

"Now don't get upset, let's leave the phone unanswered for awhile, and try to review the messages as they come in. Maybe you can try to reach Lieutenant Davis, uh, I mean 'our friend Richard' to inform him that the media frenzy is continuing."

"I already did," I replied, "but his office said that he was out, so I left a message for him; maybe you can keep a look out for his return call."

"Lieutenant Davis didn't give us a time when the District Attorney would do our interviews," Chris responded, again unable to refer to the Lieutenant as Richard.

"I still have a few more people to call in Miami, and I want to reach them before we head into the weekend. I'll be downstairs."

Chris watched me go downstairs into my inner sanctum. She knew the garden outside and my private office were where I was most comfortable, sitting or working among my treasured surroundings. She also knew, and disapproved of the fact that I would light up one of my favorite cigars in order to do some serious thinking in quiet.

Later, in the early afternoon, after talking with several more folks in Miami, I was ready for a little time in the gardens. Time spent with the flowers and assorted plants and shrubs was definitely my therapy. My mind could just go blank as I pinched, and pulled and cut, and generally fussed with the gardens. From experience I knew there was no way to pull just one weed. One would definitely lead to two, then three and so on.

Looking around I realized the grass hadn't been cut this week. It would wait. In fact most people cut their lawns too short during mid-summer anyhow. The grass at this point, though high, looked good. My mowing activity, another favorite ritual, usually brought comments from neighbors passing by on the side walk. I was very proud of my old push mower, which was environmentally correct; however I was often reminded that the ever-present cigar nullified any points I might make because of this manual mower. Invariably some one shouted up to the effect, "Do you know how much faster that job would go if you had a power mower?" This always amused me, and my favorite rejoinder was always two fold.

"Where am I going that I have to do this job in a hurry; and do you know how many boring meetings I sat through over the years, and had my mind wander to this day; no deadlines, no crises, and no problems? This is the pay off man! I don't care how long this job takes!" As a practical matter it was not a very big lawn anyway, forty-five minutes, or getting through a cheap cigar, which ever came first.

With my cell phone nearby and a nice pitcher of lemonade carefully placed in the shade of the side porch, I took a seat and proceeded to rock awhile. Few people had the cell number. I hoped no one would call. I disliked these gadgets and had this one only as a concession to Chris. She wanted to be able to reach me at any time if she needed me. Hah! I knew it was a ploy on her part. She had given me the phone so that I could reach her if I needed her. It was a gloriously warm and lazy summer afternoon. There was always a wonderful breeze on the porch or under the trees, to provide much needed relief. "Tell me I should be someplace else," I cried to no one in particular. This is just what I had in mind when we decided to leave Miami. As they say: Asheville Chamber of Commerce weather!

Oh, oh, a noise coming from the parking lot. Who could that be? We had no check-ins this afternoon.

Son of a gun, it's a large white van, with a dish and stenciled neatly on the side the words Channel 13 TV, Your Friendly Local Mountain TV Station. Damn they're pushing their luck now. Here comes the camera man, and, to my surprise, Jennifer Bother, herself, the anchor of the five o'clock news. Boy, this is a treat; Ms. Bother was by reputation a very aggressive, in-your-face type of reporter. It seemed a little strange that she would come out on this call herself, and not send some underling. I walked down to greet her before she got much further.

I was particularly conscious of how attractive, make that pretty, Ms. Bother was. Boy she's some knock-out. TV doesn't do her any favors at all. She was much more imposing in person. Her honey blonde hair was blowing gently in the breeze, and her outfit was preppy: blue button down shirt, cuffed tan trousers and loafers, no socks or stockings. I thought I did remember reading somewhere of her New England Ivy League background. Pretty blue eyes, high cheekbones, and a well proportioned mouth filled out the picture. I took in all this in a matter of seconds. Don't tell me that TV people don't succeed because of looks. There was no question that the isolated age discrimination lawsuit brought by aging female anchors, or even male correspondents, had a good deal of merit. Ms. Bother was clearly the complete package, and no doubt she knew it. Asheville was surely just a necessary short stop-over for her before her move to a larger market.

"Hold it right there, Ms. Bother, I really do not want a media circus on my property."

"You can't deny the news, Mr. Loving, maybe you can blow off one of our young production associates, but not me. You do know who I am right?"

"Yes, I do," I murmured, slightly taken back by those aggressive remarks.

"And you must know Mr. Loving, that our viewers and all the people of Asheville have a right to the news. It is our understanding that a particularly heinous homicide occurred here yesterday, and I have pictures of the crime scene tape that was here yesterday, just in case you'd like to see it to refresh your memory. We know it was a homicide, and that's news, and that's our business."

In some ways you had to admire Ms. Bother's single-mindedness; yet there was no way I would accommodate her. "If you have any questions, direct them to Lieutenant Davis, downtown. We have no comment here, so please get back in your van and hit the road."

I could imagine Chris shaking her head with her 'Oh, that was good, Ed,' look on her face if she heard me. "Ms. Bother, I think I've been clear from the beginning; but let me repeat: we don't want any kind of circus-like atmosphere on this property, and particularly, we do not want our guests privacy intruded upon."

"Are you saying you won't talk to us?" This was crisp and sharp. "Clearly, we, along with the police department and everyone in this entire neighborhood know something happened here yesterday, and you won't talk to us?"

"I think you have it." I said. "The answer is 'yes' I won't talk to you. I repeat, one more time, please get any details from Lieutenant Davis."

"You can't do this, Mr. Loving, you are obstructing the public's right to news, and you seriously offended me; I'm just trying to do my job. We'll see who gets the last word here. Let me invite you to listen to my show tonight. I'm sure you know it's the five o'clock news. Between you and me, buster, I can't wait!"

Chris appeared in the window of the Butler's Pantry. I could see she was upset by what she'd seen and heard. I knew she'd think I could have handled the situation better, but this woman was something else. I bit my tongue, but the term 'a real bitch' sprang to mind. I knew we'd know more when the news came on at five o'clock.

The news entourage was leaving in an unceremonious fashion, and I could now go back to the porch. Ms. Bother did turn around a few times on her way to the van, and I bet it was not to wish me well. Most probably it wasn't a good idea to confront her like that. "The public's right to know", hogwash! She was an ambitious gal toiling away in a really small market, and here was a chance for her to get a local exclusive, and maybe some good national coverage, too. What a shame, I really felt for her. I was sure she'd do her best at five o'clock to lambaste me. Fortunately, the camera man never had filmed our exchange. In her outrage at me, she forgot to turn around and face the camera. She was making sure she stared right at me. We'll see!

Going back inside, I told Chris my side of the little incident with Ms. Bother.

"I know, Ed, I heard you through the dining room window. You really handled that situation well, and we should get a fair share of coverage tonight on the early news. You can just bet Ms. Bother will have something nice to say." I knew that when Chris was that facetious, she was upset and probably right to be worried.

What I did care about though, was some information I had received from Miami, and how, or if, I would share it with Lieutenant Davis.

"Let me go over to the cottage and change, maybe take a little lie down. I'll be back in time to watch the news with you and get ready for wine and cheese. There's plenty of time, plenty of time."

I laid down on the bed in our cottage and tried to read, I really did. But before I knew it, the book was on the floor, my glasses were next to the pillow and it was already quarter past five in the afternoon.

I combed my hair, slapped some water on my face, and headed over to the inn. Chris had everything under control - cheese, wine, crackers, fruit, music, etc. She also had a rather bemused expression on her face.

"My hero! You missed a good news program at five o'clock, channel thirteen, Ms. Jennifer Bother herself. I'm not going to repeat what she said, mainly because I think the woman is a certified bitch. But rather, if my instincts are still good, I think you will be getting enough calls later tonight, and enough of an ear full from most people in this town. Remember, honey, we're partners and I love you very much." Chris had that little twinkle in her eye. It must have been some lead in on the 5 o'clock news.

The cars were back. The sounds of returning guests, laughter in the hallways and on the stairs, doors opening and closing, conversations in the butler's pantry, everyone had returned, and as usually happened could not wait to share their experiences of the day.

"Take the first shift, Chris, let me answer the phone."

"'Polite Society', this is Ed, can I help you?"

"Are you crazy!? Ed, are you there? Have you lost your mind?"

"Jerry so nice to hear from you, I hope you're having a nice evening a well."

"Ed, please, did you watch the five o'clock news?"

"No, I didn't," I replied. "I was busy, but I bet I can guess at a large part of it."

"Don't be cute Ed; you've outsmarted yourself on this one. Not only did your friend Ms. Bother do a hatchet job on you as an irresponsible local business man, but she alluded to the whole Bed and Breakfast community in Asheville as tight lipped and insensitive to the rights of the 'local folks; we're interlopers at best.'"

"Ah, yes, Jerry. The same old story; 'the B&B people' are only here to take short term advantage of the city. So it seems Ms. Bother felt compelled to dust off that little old chestnut?'

"It's not funny, Ed, seriously. I've gotten calls already from some of the other bed and breakfasts. They know we're close friends, and they're upset that you'd get Channel 13 all excited with your 'flippant' and 'disrespectful' manner. Their words, I might add. That Ms. Bother did quite a number on you, and by inference, on all of us!"

"Jerry, listen to me. Did it ever occur to you or any of those 'Nervous Nelly' innkeepers in town that by virtue of Ms. Bother's tirade on the air, which I did not see, you understand, she is personally magnifying the situation herself? I think you would agree, it's for her own motives and aggrandizement! If you get any more calls, Jerry ...and oh yeah, I hope you're not letting folks in on what we've told you ... Jerry, talk to me!"

"Of course not. Ellen and I would not violate the confidence you have in us."

I went on, "Now, let me start again. If you get any more calls, or whatever, refer all inquires to Lieutenant Richard Davis, Asheville Police Dept. Can you do that for me?"

"Yes, of course I can," Jerry countered. "In fact, that's exactly what I did when Stan Eager called."

"Oh, that's great. Jerry, you're telling me that Stan Eager, the Executive Director of the Chamber of Commerce called you, and not me?"

"He sure did," snapped Jerry, "and I told him to call you or Lieutenant Davis. I told him I wasn't a part of this."

By now I knew that the media and public consumption of Tydings' death had been pretty well botched up. For some reason Lieutenant Davis had not returned my call yet. I needed his help in providing a spin on this, so everyone will calm down. Chris and I haven't made out our list of calls yet; it didn't seem to me to be necessary so soon. But then, what do I know. Lieutenant Davis and the District Attorney had better get on this pretty soon. What the deuce were they waiting for?

Just then I heard laughter from the den. Oh, yeah, I have to get inside and help Chris with the guests. Let me get back to some normalcy. At that, the phone rang and I picked it up reflexively on the first ring.

"Ed, Richard Davis here. Sorry I didn't get back sooner, but I spent the afternoon in Greensboro. I've been out of pocket all day. I'm sure you want to talk about our good friend Ms. Jennifer Bother. Well, to put your mind at ease, she was completely off base in her ranting and raving on this evening's program. It was ill advised, unprofessional, and down right hateful. She has been contacted personally by the Mayor, our police chief and the owner of the station. You don't have to worry about her anymore. The District Attorney will have a prepared statement for the ten o'clock news that we hope puts out any fire there. You know: tragic accident, being followed up by our local police, blah, blah, yadda, yadda, yadda; and oh yeah, the fact that you are not considered a suspect. I hope this helps, but I know a lot of damage has been done already. Are you and Chris all right?"

"Yes, we are, and Lieutenant, thanks for your support, albeit a little late. We do have a lot of unnecessary excitement among the other Bed and Breakfast owners, and my good friend Stan Eager at the Chamber, but that should be greatly alleviated by your information on the 10 o'clock news later tonight."

"What did Eager want?"

"Lieutenant, I don't know. He called a friend who referred him to me or you. I haven't heard from him so far, so you may hear from him before I do!"

"Relax, Ed, if I'm not mistaken, it's wine and cheese time at your place. Go in and do what you do best. Take care of your guests, keep them cool, and keep them here to fuel the local economy. Just like a politician, huh? You did what I asked you to do, so do not worry about Ms. Bother anymore. The next round of excitement will be if the national people descend upon us. Hopefully, the District Attorney's statement tonight will help, but remember, refer all calls to me. That'll take you off the hot seat, or hook, completely. Gotta run, talk to you later."

I must admit I did feel better now, particularly knowing Ms. Bother's chain had been yanked. But I was sure there were plenty of folks out there who were very upset about this whole thing. We'd handle it one at a time I guessed. The fact of the matter, and Lieutenant Davis, his friends the mayor, the police chief and all, couldn't dismiss it, - was that there was a homicide here. Horace Tydings was dead, and whoever was responsible was still at large.

Another telephone call; this one on the private line.

"Hello? Dad?" It was Everett's voice.

"What's going on down there? Are you and Chris all right?"

Everett and his sister Page call my wife Chris. Their mother had lived for a number of years after our divorce, when they were still in single digit ages, and used them both as weapons against me. She had insisted that "mother" was to be reserved exclusively for her. Chris, bless her heart, had spread out her wings like a mother hen, and gathered Everett and Page under them in the same way that Charles and Dianna found comfort, advice and love there. It was a credit to them all, that when my wife's ears heard "Chris" her mind and heart heard 'mom', just as the children intended.

I couldn't help but notice a little extra concern in our son's voice. Here we go again. The concerned son routine, he wants to tell me how to handle this, I thought. He was the one who was so concerned when we decided to quit our jobs and open the inn. I vividly remember the long distance conversations with him in Ottawa at that time: "You're going to do what? You're going where? Are you all right? Let me speak to Chris!" Everett was convinced the old man had lost it, and I believed he was the one most concerned for Chris's welfare at that time. I heard the same hesitant anxiety now.

"We just had a small news item up here, unconfirmed, we're told, in our early news about Horace Tydings being found dead at a bed and breakfast in Asheville. Do you know anything about it?"

At this point I wanted to get inside, and so responded to our dear son as simply as I could manage.

"No! I can't say that I do. Listen my fine boy, we are right in the middle of wine and cheese, let me call you later. How's Dawn, by the way?"

"Well, she's doing very well, and so are the girls. We'll wait for your call. So long, Dad, love you!"

That last bit, 'love you' came so easily to the kids, and to everyone but me. To me, real men do not say "I love you". My dad never said that, hell; I just knew that he did. Today, the kids rightly or wrongly have no hang-ups at all about expressing their feelings. My primary objection, if you can call it that, was that the ease with which people express their feelings, doesn't always equate to an honest or sincere feelings. I was getting better at it, I knew, it just came a little harder to me. My mother and father were just not as open about their feelings. Hell, our whole family wasn't. That's just the way I grew up. Credit those good old taciturn New England Yankee customs.

Enough! Let me get inside. No more calls please! I went in to talk to our guests a little more in depth. Based on a few calls to Miami I had some questions to clear up. I knew what I told Lieutenant Davis. Yeah, stay away; let the professionals do their job. Well, it was my inn, my reputation and in the minds of some, my neck on the line. I just wanted to help clear up some questions I had. Did I have anything to lose?

CHAPTER VII

The guests….

Friday 6 PM

Chris entertained the guests beautifully by herself for some time. They all had busy days and wanted to share.

As I entered the parlor Bill Oates and his wife Mary broke off from the larger group in the parlor to examine the old photographs of Chris's and my grandparents.

"Ed, we were just admiring these wonderful old pictures; and such lovely frames."

The pictures were from sometime about the turn of the century, the poses were so stiff and contrived, with the man seated and the wife posed dutifully standing behind him. Not particularly or politically correct in this day and age.

"Thank you, Mary. We enjoy people admiring these pictures, and various other items, some with historical interest, at least for our families. Those pictures are of Chris' and my grandparents. Here, let me show you this store ledger, right here on the mantle. Now, this dates back to 1837, and as you can see survived everything since, except a four year old named Page who thought it appropriate to use it as a coloring book."

"Oh no," murmured Mary, seeing the rich splashes of color on several pages.

"This is the store's journal from Loving's General Store in Colebrook, New Hampshire. Chris and I were up there a few years ago and saw the location, right in town on Main Street, but the store itself burned down a long time ago. The store was owned by my grandfather's brother.

"Just look at some of these entries," Mary exclaimed. "The name of the customer, the date and the cost; see this one, October 13, 1838, Thomas Carlyle, 1/2 dozen eggs: 6 cents, 1 pint of rum: 10 cents, 1/2 tin of tobacco: 15 cents, and look, here's 4 pounds of sugar for 50 cents. What fun to go through this old ledger."

"What an order for old Tom," chuckled Bill. "What do you think he was up to that day?"

I enjoyed this. From the secretary I grabbed another book. "Let me show you another little treasure I discovered in my father's papers after he died a few years ago. It's Primer on the Duties and Responsibilities of a Justice of the Peace in New Hampshire. The book was published in 1824, and the flyleaf has an inscription of ownership by one Daniel Rogers, September 1830."

I heard someone shout "You have such great books everywhere!" The voice was Sherry Greenlee's who was coming over to join us. Her enthusiasm was infectious.

"I really like those large coffee table books you placed upstairs in our room. They're a little bulky for bedtime reading, but great to just leaf through, particularly when my friend over there is hogging the bathroom."

"I heard that", shouted John from across the room.

Sherry looked up at me smiling. "Ed you and Chris certainly have created a special place here, we feel so comfortable and at ease. You two are just perfect."

"Why, thanks, Sherry."

"I think so too," chimed in Mary. "I should tell you that Bill and I have talked about owning a bed and breakfast. We really can't afford one yet. We're still working our butts off to stay ahead, but sometime in the future I hope we can realize our dream. And if we do, we'll try to be just like you and Chris."

"Wow." I said to Chris "Give these ladies some more wine. Seriously Mary, Sherry, thank you for your kind comments.

"Hold on friend," said Chris. "These people have to get out to eat. Let's make their dinner reservations for them and get everyone on their way."

I thought not for the first time, that Chris had a wonderful way of getting my attention, and of knowing what was appropriate for the occasion. For me, I guess, it was just too easy to think 'Party Time'. You just had to love her. Of course no more wine. We wanted people to drive safely to their dining spots and back with no unpleasant incidents.

"Are you all set for dinner, Bill?" I asked.

"Yeah, Mary went upstairs to get a sweater and we're off as soon as she comes down."

"Say, didn't you mention earlier that you were CFO of North American Trading in Orlando?"

"I'm not really sure I did, but now that you mention it I was there until about six months ago, when I was unceremoniously terminated. I've pretty much been on the ropes ever since, but we have a pretty good cash reserve and I'm being selective on my next position. I've already had some very fine offers, and you know what, I'm a little 'snake bit' right now. I'll be all right; I'm just taking my time to sort everything out.

"I'm sorry; I didn't mean to hit a sore spot. I'm just curious now; if I recall, didn't Tydings take over that company last year?"

"You're right, Ed. I hate to say this, but since you brought it up, I did see him check in late the other night, and of course heard him blundering up the stairs. I told Mary that I really felt like checking out. I didn't think I could face that guy without causing a scene; doing or saying something I know I would regret later."

"I know what you mean, how he can get under your skin."

Bill pulled me aside, and dropped his voice. "That's not really the worst of it. My dad had been with the company for twenty-seven years. He was the VP in charge of Sales, and he was let go too, shortly after the takeover. It happened only a year before he was due to retire."

"Oh, Bill, I'm so sorry. I hate to hear stories like that."

"It gets worse. Based on the new policies, that no one was aware of except Tydings and his new henchmen directors, this left my dad not only without a job, but more seriously, without his pension! And get this, Tydings had the gall to tell me we both were expendable because the company's pension fund was in trouble, 'under-funded' he called it, and he had to save money. My mother died shortly thereafter. To this day my dad blames Tydings for her untimely death. He's convinced that if he had his pension he would have been able to get better medical care for her."

"There's probably some truth in that."

Bill went on, obviously getting more upset as he continued: "Imagine trying to pay for a decent nursing home on nothing but your social security and modest savings over the years. She developed severe depression and dementia. Dad couldn't take care of her himself. I did my best to help financially. To top it off, Dad finally had to put her in a horrible place, and it damn near killed him to do it. Dad is now a greeter at damned Wal-Mart – for minimum wage! Nice family story, wouldn't you say?"

I had no reply. I wondered how much a man could take. Did Bill Oates take things into his own hands when he realized that Tydings was here? Could Bill have murdered John Tydings? I thought there was a strong motive here, with a capital "M"!

"Ah, here comes Mary. Ed, maybe we can chat later when we return from dinner. I have so many conflicting emotions right now. On the one hand I really thought of calling my dad, much as one would do after winning the lottery, and yet this conflicts so with my Christian values."

Is he putting me on? I wondered. Here this creep Tydings ruined his father's retired life, contributed to the death of his mother, and put Bill on the unemployment line for the last six months, and he considers that his quite natural feelings of glee about Tydings death put him in conflict with his Christian teachings. That's quite a lot to swallow.

Mary was waiting patiently by the front door. We walked over to her.

"Have a good dinner, you two, enjoy your evening, and maybe we'll see you later.

"Thanks, Ed." In unison they added, "Give our goodnights to Chris!"

I returned to the parlor to find just the Greenlees engrossed in a small pocket sized book. As I get closer I recognized it, and remembered how neat both Chris and I thought it was when we purchased it earlier this year in Williamsburg. Ah yes. It was a reproduction of a little book by George Washington. On the heels of my conversation with Bill, it was quite a coincidence to see this book now. I read from the book's introduction:

"At the age of fourteen, George Washington wrote down one hundred ten rules under the title, *Rules of Civility and Decent Behavior*

In Company and Conversation. These rules were drawn from an English translation of a French book of maxims and were intended to polish manners, keep alive the best affections of the heart, impress the obligation of moral virtues, teach how to treat others in social relations and above all, incubate the practice of a perfect self control."

I couldn't have said it better.

"These are truly words to live by; everything in moderation."

I thought, not for the first time, the world really hadn't progressed very far.

"Aren't you two going to eat?" I asked John and Sherry Greenlee as they appeared to be settling in for the evening in the den.

"We had a late lunch at the Biltmore Estate, and some very good ice cream after that in a frozen custard shop at the Grove Arcade. I think we've had it for today. We can get a good night's sleep and an early start tomorrow, at Bele Chere downtown." Sherry explained.

"Besides, we want to finish up the picture puzzle in here." John added. "We love doing jigsaw puzzles and yours is set up so neatly, and is so inviting. We're okay, don't worry about us."

Chris had already gone over to our cottage at the rear of the inn to begin our dinner. So I was left to clean up the vestiges of wine and cheese, and answer any telephone messages left during the past two hours. I also needed to fire up a Monte Cristo and have a good 'rock' on the side porch before my dinner.

"Say, did you see where Phil and Barbara Kerry went off to?" I ask Sherry as I headed for the porch.

"Haven't seen them in a while," she replied. "Really didn't get much of a chance to visit with them tonight. They were here, and then they were gone. I don't think they even had a glass of wine!"

How strange. While I believed that Wine and Cheese was such a great time, it turned out that some guests could live without it. Chris told me our feelings go a little deeper than that. I've heard other bed and breakfast owners talk about it as well. We all seemed to have a penchant for seeking and responding to positive reinforcement. We were like little kids who wanted their heads patted constantly and had trouble when guests just accepted things, without kind words or plaudits for the innkeepers. Oh, well!

That was what it must have been with the Kerrys! They simply had early reservations and had to go. I just couldn't shake a feeling though, about Phil. He seemed overly distracted on the porch yesterday, and at breakfast, and he and Barbara hadn't entered into our common conversations. What was annoying me was that I knew that name, Kerry. It bothered me that I didn't recall how I knew it. It would come to me. Maybe one of my calls to Miami would shake it loose.

I ducked my head into the den, "I'll be on the porch for a while if you people need anything, and then I'll be over in the cottage. Maybe I'll see you later."

As I headed off I heard quite clearly, "Enjoy your cigar, Ed."

A little later, walking over to the cottage, I stopped go stare at the koi pond. What was it? Maybe a day and a half ago, when that jerk Tydings 'did a Brodie' into my pond. And now it was probably a homicide. The words most used since have been suspicious death. As opposed to what, I wonder? No, that's not it. It's why? Why would someone simply wait in a garden with a slim to no chance of not being seen to kill someone? What are the chances of finding someone so all alone behind a bed and breakfast? And then, after the deed, take off without being seen. I was told that Tydings had all of his jewelry accounted for, as well as a wad of bills in his pocket. It didn't appear to be a robbery. It was so strange that the only noise I heard was the splash. I just kept coming back to a possible scenario: someone familiar with our schedule; when guests take off, and all that. Or of course, a present guest, who can easily come and go on the property with no questions asked. This narrowed it down considerably, and like it or not, Bill Oates' experience with Tydings gave him plenty of motive for mayhem. For some reason, I didn't like him for it though.

"What do I smell?" I asked as I walked into the cottage.

"Onions, onions and more sautéed onions. Pan grilled steak, smothered onions, mashed potatoes, and green beans." Chris replied.

"Hallelujah!"

I often joked about our separate quarters giving us the ability to cook onions, have domestic disagreements, yell at the referees on TV and not feel at all guilty about a cat. There was no doubt that having our living space in a separate cottage gave us a sense of freedom and privacy that few other innkeepers in town enjoyed. We never feel that we are tied to the inn, or prisoners in our own home as others say they do. I had to give Chris a lot of credit for insisting that the original garage be expanded and renovated for our personal space. The one month we spent in one of the guest rooms with the other rooms full of guests, waiting for our cottage to be completed, did away with any misgiving I might have had about the added expense.

. "You read my mind, honey; some good red meat with an ice cold beer for me and a little merlot for you? Who's got it better?"

We sat down, said our grace, and dug in.

I repeated for Chris everything Bill Oates shared with me. She was of a similar mind that it certainly could be a motive, and he fit the idea that a guest seemed the most likely, and easiest of murderers to move around the property without causing any concern. It all came back to Tydings. How one man could so disrupt a family? Whenever I went down this path, I couldn't help arriving at a sense of justice in this awful tragedy.

Chris asked if there were any calls of any importance.

"Not really, a few brochure requests, a couple of hang ups. If you snooze, you loose, as they say." There was no question that most everyone wanted to talk with a real person, particularly at a Bed and Breakfast where we were selling the personal touch and return to concerned service for the guests. Unfortunately, I agreed, and had been known my self to hang up on a Bed and Breakfast if I got a recording.

Chris savored the last drops of her wine. My steak was gone; I pretty much inhaled it!

"What a great meal."

We had to work a little on stretching a good meal out. Chris, of course, was much better than I, but sitting down to a good home cooked meal, steak, chicken, turkey, whatever, became something of a mission for me. It represented something to be accomplished. The fork was always in motion. One of our diet books had the suggestion of putting one's fork down between bites, and of course this would lead to a much more desirable rate of food intake, and would lead to more desirable digestion. Phooey!

I told Chris, "Well, we've gotten calls from each of the kids. Apparently some news services have picked up the story and by now it's national news. They all wanted to talk to us, their father in particular, about Mr. John Tydings."

"I can appreciate that. Well, who goes first, do we throw the four names in a hat, or do we go by age? How about by the number of miles away from Asheville?" replied Chris.

Over the years we had impressed upon the kids a spirit of independence in pursuing a career no matter where it took them. I knew that Chris was not as positive about this as I was; and now I too wished they were a least within a two or three hour drive. But no, we had Charles, an engineer and sales manager in San Francisco, where it would take a goodly supply of TNT to blast him out of the 'city by the bay'. Then Page was in Houston along with two children and her husband, Vince, who was seeking to make his living in the construction business. Everett had his own growing accounting firm near Ottawa and his wife not only a partner in their firm, but a career as the 'go to' expert on ethics and standards for CGA Canada. Dianna was an executive with United Way in Palm Beach, following her initial career in commercial real estate lending. All were gainfully employed, doing well and at least through today, not looking to the old man for a dime!

A dime!

I'd completely forgotten. Tonight was poker night at Bob's house.

"Oh, no!"

I had to admit that there was one aspect to my life here that I had yet to fill in, and that was my cherished "male bonding." In Miami and New York, as well as through my athletic school years, this seemingly barbaric custom of men getting together in 'macho drag' to act on most occasions like deranged teenagers was dear to me. The camaraderie was a necessary part of being. The cigars, the bad jokes, the mindless teasing and of course the drinking were necessary evils of existence, beyond any mere rites of passage. And now, I'd forgotten the poker game, held at Bob's because his wife Trudy doesn't object, at least not too strenuously in front of us, to cigars, cigarettes and pipe smoke in their basement playroom. I forgot to call. I hope they have enough hands. Truth be told, the peanuts, chips and cold beer, were an enormous magnet to "the game", as are the sandwiches at 10:30 to 11:00 PM, made by Trudy. So, bottom line for this day was my card game was shot and my golf tournament was shot.

Quite selfishly, I was still concerned about the tragedy and its impact on the inn and future business. Worst case scenario: The investigation would center on the inn, and no doubt our attention to security. The consequences need not be explained, Chris and I would be held directly responsible for the Tydings death. The loss of business would certainly be disastrous, but long term and more significantly it would affect our life here and ultimately the value of the property.

"I can't think of this anymore." I told Chris.

And wouldn't you know: I had an unused and unpaid for room for four days, during Bele Chere. What a pity! That put Tydings demise in perspective for me, but I wouldn't share these thoughts with anyone.

CHAPTER VIII

The kids....

Friday: 7:30 – 11 PM

"Everett, my boy, it's Dad. Chris is on the line as well. We wanted to fill you in on the events here of the last two days."

"That's great, Dad, but let me do this; I can get Dianna and Page and Charles on a conference call and call you back. That way we all can hear it together and can all ask you questions."

"Fair enough, but do it right away," I added.

"Give me a break, Dad; it could take a few minutes."

"Okay, talk to you later." Leave it to Everett to have a better idea. He was our late bloomer, but now he was always so willing to please, and so quick to take the initiative; always a better idea. At this point in life we generally serenaded him with a drawn out version of 'Mr. Wonderful'. Every family has one!

Chris thought a minute and said: "We should tell them everything. They're not just our children, but they're our best friends as well. I see no reason to hold back anything, and not tell them everything we know. Besides, I really haven't thought it through enough to think of what to leave out."

"I agree; we'll just wait for the call back. I'll be outside for a smoke."

It was a lovely night, no wind, just as calm as could be. Our nightly serenade of cicadas hasn't started yet. I wanted to just sit here close to the door, where I could hear Everett's return call. It was time for one of my 'cheap puppies'. I might have to leave it and I wouldn't want to waste a good cigar.

A moment later a car came into the parking area. I thought it was a pretty early return for any of our guests. The Greenlees stayed in so yes, it was the Kerrys. Whoa, that's quite a door slam. Since I was pretty much covered in shadows I'd just sit here quietly.

I saw that Phil wasn't waiting for Barbara; he was well ahead of her. The body language here didn't look too reflective of the end of a pleasant evening.

"I don't want to discuss it, Barbara. Let it go, please, for my sake."

"Oh, Phil, you must!"

Barbara caught up to him and I didn't hear anything more. Those two didn't look like happy campers. I wondered what he didn't want to discuss, and why did Barbara think he must? It was probably just a young couple's disagreement. It was much too soon to jump to any conclusions.

Ah! There's the phone. We'd get on with the important things.

"Dad, Chris? It's Everett. We're all on except for Charlie. He's on a trip, won't be back until Tuesday according to his Diane." The 'his Diane' made the distinction between Charlie's wife and his sister. Even the ladies middle names were the almost the same- Marie and Maria.

"Hi, Mom, Ed; Dad, Chris," came a chorus from Dianna and Page.

"Hi," I greeted everyone. "Now that we're all together let me bring you up to date about what you may or may not be seeing on TV or reading in the papers. Everett, you reach Charlie as soon as you can, and report what we say."

"No problem, Dad, will do.'

Over the next twenty minutes I recounted in enough details the events of the last few days, with some details provided by Chris. I highlighted the facts that I was not considered a suspect, and that the local District Attorney and Chief of Detectives of the Asheville Police were prepared to state the same in an interview on tonight's local 10 o'clock news. It should hit the wires later tonight and be national news in tomorrow's media outlets.

"All right! That's good!" they shouted together.

"Now, first and foremost," Everett spoke for the group, "how are you two doing? Can we help; are you OK for support with your friends there? Do you want us to come down, over and up?"

Everett meant literally; and I did find the amusement right away: down from Ottawa, over from Houston, up from Palm Beach! The respective home towns of the kids, not counting Charles in San Francisco!!

Chris and I reminded them of our dear friends Ellen and Jerry across the street and several of my golfing buddies at the club, as well as Chris' network of close girlfriends.

"We're over the initial phase of discovering the homicide, the public airing of the tragedy, my peculiar involvement with the victim and lastly, the rush of being a 'person of interest', if you will. These issues are now far removed and in the background. Thank God." I told them.

"The fact of the matter," I continued, "and I need not remind everyone, I'm sure, is that there is a killer on the loose. This by itself is unnerving. There appears to be no robbery motive in the incident, so the reason for this evil act remains a mystery. Perhaps there is another target; or it could be just some crazy passing through, but I don't believe that."

I didn't share with the kids my nagging suspicion that a guest or a familiar face around the inn, was very likely responsible. On this score Chris and I were aware that there were extra patrolmen now, keeping an eye on the property, as well as an extra police cruiser patrolling throughout the night.

"Is it safe? Do you feel uneasy about going out, particularly at night?" Page and Dianna were definitely closing in on a little hysteria.

"Calm down you two, let's not get paranoid. We are fine; in fact I was just outside in the garden before you called."

"Having another cigar?" the girls cried in harmony.

"Seriously everyone, Chris and I feel safe here. We believe the events were an anomaly, however no less mysterious and no less tragic. "

"At this point we have many side issues that over the near and long term will gain in increasing importance."

"Has anyone from Tydings' organization gotten in touch, Dad?" asked Everett. "I mean, he always fancied himself El super major domo; nothing happened in his corporations without his approval. I remember hearing about him while I was in high school in Miami, how his executives were frightened to the bone of him and wouldn't do you know what without asking his permission."

"I agree, Everett, that most of what you heard was probably true."

"I'll tell you this too, Dad, I bet there isn't much sadness in the Miami business community, or for that matter, even in the Tydings organization. How much you want to bet, Dad? I mean the guy was a real sleaze bag!"

"Everett", responded Chris, "regardless of one's feelings, and perhaps ones' reputation, the man is dead. A rather inglorious death at that, and we as a family can at least show the world in general, our unified sympathy."

"Even I can't do much of that honey," I said. "I know what you're saying, and Lord, I'd like to be more sympathetic, but I must admit I'm generally with Everett on this one. I would be a bald faced hypocrite if I didn't secretly take some satisfaction in what happened."

"Ed, my dear partner, you better put a lid on those comments, immediately," cautioned Chris. "This entire episode has been no fun at all. And you kids, what was just discussed, is not what we really think, and is not what the Loving family is all about. You all have been very kind and considerate to call, and we thoroughly appreciate hearing from you. We have had a tragic death on our property and we must now deal with it. Statements like your father just made, are certainly not very Christian-like and more importantly could very easily re-kindle the supposition that Dad had a role in the homicide. So, let's agree that there will be no more loose talk by any family member."

"Mom," interrupted Dianna, "you know I took over the Corporate Gift-giving division of United Way here in Palm Beach. Mr. John Tydings personally cancelled several pledges this year from his existing companies as well as from a few new companies he recently acquired."

"Oh, honey, I'm so sorry. I know how hard you worked on that campaign." Chris interrupted.

"Thanks, Mom." Dianna continued. "The stock answer has been simply 'difficult times and less than anticipated earnings'. I have personally been contacted by several of the executives, who I worked with this year and last. They apologized profusely for these cancellations. The men were really embarrassed to have to go back on their word. Tydings, I was told, always has the final say. Speculation is that he simply increased his own salary by the amounts of the voided pledges. I hear what you say Mom, but I think I too would be hypocritical in any feeling of sympathy. And I have something to admit as well. When I heard of his death, it was with great effort that I suppressed an impulse to immediately make contact with these same executives to see if the policies could now be counter-manned."

"Oh, Dianna, let everything work its own way out", replied Chris. As for me, I bit my lip, and kept my mouth shut….for a change.

Dawn, Everett's wife, was now on the line too, and was happy to hear the Chief of Detectives assessment for my lack of motive and therefore no real suspicion of my involvement. Dawn was a real knock-out, a slender and attractive brunette, who if necessary, would stop the world to protect her family. We all recognized her strong opinions, usually well thought out and based on fact. I knew this, if anyone was ever in need of a strong ally, Dawn was high on my list.

"Do you have any theories, Dad?" asked Dawn.

"Not really, dear girl, but as I say, we are into a few more issues other than my being ruled out as a suspect. Namely, near term, is there a killer running around loose, and is he or she going to return for further havoc? The experts tell us that with each passing day, the assailant's trail and any associated clues, gets colder and colder. Also, we hope the sensationalism of our local media doesn't put a real damper on future *Polite Society* reservations. Or, for that matter, in the larger picture, hurt tourism in general for Asheville, itself. Add to this, any repercussions of Tydings death and his related interests, namely his children or hired gun attorneys, looking to stir up trouble. We have enough issues to keep us entertained over the near term."

"Don't forget about us, out here in Houston," chimed in Page and her husband, Vince. "We did tell you yesterday that as fate would have it, Tydings Enterprises, an arm of the overall empire, bought Vince's company a few months ago. At the time there were various and sundry verbal assurances that all things would basically stay the same. And with Tydings muscle of an empire, and financial wherewithal, several of Vince's pet projects could actually proceed ambitiously. Well, the early part of this week, the real facts of life started to come out. Vince's company was essentially going to be broken up into several parts which would then be brokered out for sale. It was explained that the parts were deemed to be more valuable than the company as a whole."

Vince broke in: "It's clearly the pension funds; they are very valuable assets that somehow are being incorporated into the Tydings organization's holding company. Word is the entire Houston team is slated to be cut loose."

"Page, honey, Vince, we are so sorry. This is too terrible for you. Come visit us, you both need a vacation, a change of scenery. I need to see my grandchildren and give them reassuring hugs. Please say you will come."

"We'd love to, and I wouldn't rule it out", said Page, "but we think Vince's best interests lie in trying to relocate quickly." Quite cynically, Page continued, "Our credit card and mortgage company don't really want to know about our cash flow problems. They just want to be paid."

At that, I couldn't resist trying to lighten her mood with a funny story from my former career. "Page, you remind me of one of my favorite stories about banking. It concerns the guy who fretted and stewed for days until his wife asked about his problem. He told her that basically, they were broke and could not pay their loans at the bank. She cheerfully replied, 'Honey, that's easy, simply call the bank and tell them you can't pay. Now it's their problem, and you won't have to worry anymore.'"

"I know, Dad, we've heard that one before. Seriously; we think Vince should be in a position to hit the pavement right away. He has made many friends, and has several excellent contacts in the construction business. And, let's not forget, there is a chance now, however ghoulish it may sound, that Tydings death could be a blessing in disguise, for us. Perhaps his executives, with the ability to do their own planning now, will re-think the value of Vince's company. We can only hope."

I thought of the amazing dynamics that were put into play yesterday, with the death of Horace Tydings. At least for this family. It appeared that good things could emanate from his premature passing. How many other personal stories were there? How many other futures and well-beings now were in the balance due to the absence of Horace Tydings?

I didn't share it aloud with anybody, but I did know the reaction in Miami among several colleagues upon hearing of Tydings' death was: "There is a God!"

"So, guys, I'm tired, it's late, and I have to go back over to the inn to lock up."

"Yes, Ed," said Dianna, "you have to walk the grounds, and have your last cigar of the day. You can't fool us."

"Say, Dad?" asked Everett "On a less dramatic note, I hope this doesn't change our plans for this year's golf odyssey."

For the past two years, Everett brought two buddies down from Ottawa during the month of August for a week of nothing but golf. Thirty-six holes of golf a day, all the cigars one can handle, and a rousing game of Hearts at night after dinner, until the first person dozes off, (usually me.) It proved to be a wonderful time spending a solid week with Everett and his friends in our home. We play several golf courses in the mountain area, even though our Country Club was so convenient. They usually put up a squawk that I had an advantage at my club...... probably true. The real secret though, and one that works with the younger men every time, is simply to 'talk' to them. The 'needle' was what it was generally called. As I said, it worked every time.

"No, I don't think so, Everett, this should be cleared up in plenty of time", I said with more confidence than I felt. Forget it, son, start making your plans, and don't forget.... tell your friends to bring money."

"Thanks, Dad" he replied, with just a hint of a chuckle.

"All right, you guys are now plugged in, your mother and I are fine, I'm not considered a suspect and our present guests have indicated that they will stay with us through the weekend. As we discussed, this whole episode created problems for us, and we have to work our way through them. You all be good, kiss the grandkids for us, Page and Dawn, and in September or October, maybe we can all get together here. Put it on your calendars; we'll close the inn and everyone can come for as long as you can get away. Plan on it, your mother will be heartbroken if you say no." That always got them I thought, along with the ever so slight enticement of sending them all plane tickets. Worked every time!

"Good night all, pleasant evenings, and as your Grandmother Florence used to say: "Remember, God sees you." We disconnected the phone, but not the caring.

"I think that went well," I offered to Chris.

"Yes, I guess so, though I really wish you would keep your opinions of Mr. Tydings to yourself. I hate to hear you make those off the cuff remarks. Let's just let sleeping dogs lie."

"You bet, babe, my lips are now sealed."

"If only that were true." Chris sighed.

A little later, bravely sitting on my favorite bench by the koi pond, with a prized Cohiba fired up, I tried to focus on several aspects of the last two days. For some reason, I began to hone in on the possibility that one of our present guests is involved.

A car pulled into the parking area. It was the Oates back from dinner. After a little bit of trouble, Bill Oates extricated himself from the passenger seat, and came weaving across the gravel. Safely navigating the three steps down from the parking area, he stumbled over to where I was sitting. Mary Oates followed him closely.

"Ed, my boy, good to see you! What a great evening! We had a wonderful meal at The Greenery. Unbelievable wine selection."

And, it looks like you made a sizeable dent in the wine cellar, I thought to myself.

Bill Oates continued, "I feel great. Boy, it's quiet out here. Why don't we have a party?"

"Shhhhh! You'll wake the neighborhood," said Mary through clenched teeth. "I think it's best for us to get upstairs and into bed."

Bill wanted none of that, "Just hold your horses, woman. Say, Ed is this where our mutual friend went in? Just where did you find him?"

"Bill!" cried Mary. She grabbed him by the belt and pulled him toward the library steps. Bill wasn't finished.

"You know, Ed, I told you earlier about my family's involvement with Tydings. Well, I was thinking during dinner that there's a certain justice in everything. Things have a way of working out. I'm not a damn bit sorry about 'poor' Horace Tydings. And I got news for you; I don't think anybody is going to lose any sleep over his death. I'm going upstairs, I've said my piece; see you all in the morning."

"Goodnight Bill, Mary." I said with some relief.

By myself again, the thought occurs to me once again: Was there anyone who was feeling sorrow over Tydings death? What a legacy! A man gets killed, and so far, everyone I talk to seemed to be elated. Did whoever do this think of it as murder, or just a different form of justice?

How was the person responsible to be judged? Interesting. Could one mount a convincing case that the assailant was actually doing the greater good? But no, killing is killing and no one person has the right to be judge and executioner; no matter how tempting.

CHAPTER IX

Chamber of Commerce....

Saturday 3:45 AM

"What is that?" We both jumped up out of a sound sleep.

"Is that the phone?"

Even half asleep I felt a dread in answering. Nothing good comes from a ringing phone at 3:45 in the morning. I looked at Chris, shrugged my shoulders, and anxiously picked up the phone.

"Everett, this is Fire Chief Adams. Sorry to call at this hour but we're responding to a brush and tree fire up at Spring Point. I know you've done some nice work up there for the Chamber, that little rustic cabin and all, so I thought you might want to be advised of the situation."

I had been recovering slowly, but now I was fully awake. "Thanks, Chief. You say a tree and brush fire?"

"Well my first truck on the scene called that to me. Just off the Blue Ridge Parkway, a little section above Spring Point, maybe five or six hundred yards from your cabin. I'm told it'll be under control in due time, so there is no real panic. But, as you know, the forest floor is quite dry from our drought, and it could flare up if we're not careful."

Ah, the beauty of a small town! In most cases it would be quite odd for the Fire Chief to call a private citizen and then to indicate a willingness to have him head that way. Usual protocol would be to order civilians to stay away. But not here, I thought as friends and fellow Rotarians made allowances for each other.

"Thanks, Chief, maybe I'll take a run up there. Has anyone else been alerted?"

"Stan Eager, your Chamber president was called, I do know that, and oh yeah, Sidney Ornstein." The dispatcher at the fire station had been busy. I wondered if I'd been called solely because the busybody dispatcher had gotten on the horn to all her family and political allies.

It annoyed me about Stan, but I didn't let the Chief know. "Thanks for the heads up. I'll see you up there within the hour."

Stan Eager was aware of my work up at the cabin; I didn't think my involvement was widely disseminated. Only a small plaque next to the door of the cabin stated that the Asheville Chamber of Commerce and the local Rotary Club provided this little way-station for people in need. Sidney Orenstein and I had worked closely with the National Park Service to clear out a spot on Spring Point, and erect a rather simple log cabin. The purpose was for it to act as a destination point for hikers, or perhaps a rudimentary shelter for a lost hunter or for that matter a shelter from the elements for anyone finding themselves in the area during a sudden storm. We had raised a good bit of money, mostly from folks who preferred to remain anonymous. We used these funds for the cabin structure, a maintenance upkeep budget for the Parks service, the clearing of a small field for picnic tables, paths and a cut out from the not too distant parkway for a few parking spaces. It really turned out well; and of course the views looking basically due west and south were awesome. Chris and I often drove up there to stop, let our golden retriever, Taffy, run around with her Frisbee for a little bit while we polished off a little Kentucky Fried Chicken. In October the entire vista, with the deciduous trees dressed in fall colors, was simply magnificent. Because it had pretty much been developed by Sidney and me, under the radar, and with little fanfare, we both felt a real proprietary interest in the spot and guarded its use quite jealously. I would hate to have Stan Eager now take any credit or strut around up there since he had opposed me and Sidney at every point of its development. To my knowledge Stan has never mentioned Spring Point to me or Sidney as being a fine result for our Recreation Development Committee. I guessed this explained my misgivings about meeting Stan up at the fire.

I explained the call to Chris who was now wide awake as well. I got up and started to dress. "Chris, honey, can you drive me up to Spring Point? You know how I hate to drive in the dark. You can drive me up and come right home. In case I run into any complications at least you'll be here for breakfast."

"Sure," Chris responded, but couldn't help a dig; "you'll do anything to get out of breakfast duties."

"Now, that's not fair."

"Okay, okay, I'll drive you up there and I'll stick around with you if you need me, to see about any complications. We'll come back together and do breakfast. I can't imagine what help you could be to the Fire Department anyway; more than likely just get in the way. You and your Chamber of Commerce cohorts!"

"Hey!"

"Alright, alright, don't get exercised. I'm just kidding. Let me get dressed, I'll be ready in a second."

We drove up to Spring Point with out incident, maybe twenty minutes away. We arrived around 4:30AM, and there were people everywhere. Park Service people, Asheville Fire and Rescue, some Asheville Police, a State Trooper or two and I recognized Father Mike McLaughlin also, standing off to the side out of the way. I know he has his own fire and police scanner for emergencies. And there, huddled around Stan Eager, were three Chamber Directors I recognized immediately. Three of the most obnoxious and self important directors, I should add. There is something more here than just a little brush fire that would bring these boys out in the middle of the night. And of course, the local newspaper and TV stations are represented and added a circus-like atmosphere to the surroundings.

"I'm leaving," shouted Chris. "Your take care, be a good boy and stay out of the way. I know you'll want to help and perhaps supervise, but just stay on the sidelines, please!" And she started to drive off.

"Of course I will. You take the fun out of everything." I shouted after her.

We jokingly had a general rule at the inn for all workmen; that Chris established the price at the reasonable going rate, but if I 'helped' or attempted to supervise, they could double the price! The workmen found this amusing and in the final analysis, had fun trying to get me involved so it would be quite beneficial, to them. Chris made sure I didn't fall for it.

"Ed, over here!" I heard my name shouted over the din. "Ed, over here!" It was Stan and his cronies.

"Hello fellas, I didn't expect to see you all up here. It appears that the fire is already under control, and we'll soon be out of here."

"Well," countered Stan, "the Chief told me he called you, and you were on your way up. I thought, when things here settle down, and it looks like they are now, we can all have a little chat about that bizarre homicide at your Bed and Breakfast property. I think that we might want to discuss media relations in general and yours in particular, as it relates to our overall tourism mission."

"What do you want to discuss first; the aggressive out of control TV bitch looking to cash in on a story at my personal expense, or the newspaper writer who without a scintilla of evidence, or hint of professional conduct who wrote a clearly inflammatory article for page one of our local rag?"

Stan turned to his buddies. "See, I told you guys he was like this. How do you think this will play in the national media? All our good marketing work has gone down the drain!"

I sized up my judge and jury. "Did any of you see the *10 O'clock News* tonight?" I waited for their reply, but there was only hemming and hawing and spluttering of "What does that have to do with anything?"

"I thought so! If you had, you would have heard the District Attorney and Chief of Police explain how ill-advised it was for anyone to suspect Ed Loving of the crime, and that I was not, I repeat, NOT to be considered under investigation. Furthermore, you would have heard our good mayor interviewed also, and heard him indicate the heavy-handed inappropriateness of our local media to rush to judgment. The Mayor apologized to me and to my family publicly and he emphasized that we should learn from this episode to be more understanding of individual citizens and must wait for facts to come out not harmful speculations. The editor of the newspaper and the TV Station Manager were also quoted as regretting the unprofessional and incompetent manner in which the story was handled by their people. Did you all catch any of that?"

They all four started to talk at the same time, much the same garbage. "I'm sorry, I didn't know", or "no one told me", or the best yet, "I really never believed any of it."

"Gentlemen," I said "let's do our best to get beyond this and get on with our lives, and live and work in Asheville, together." I thought I exhibited a statesman like manner, not that any of them agreed. But, if nothing else, I hoped my speech served to ease any lingering tension, and took the edge off any further reaction.

"Incidentally, in just twelve minutes we should have sunrise, and believe me that is a breathtaking event up here. Enjoy the rest of your day, fellas, and I'll see you all at our regularly scheduled meeting. Unless, of course, there is something else?" I couldn't restrain myself. "Were we finished, by the way, or was there a need for further discussion?"

They each looked around, over their shoulders, at their shoes, every where but at me.

"No." said Stan. "I think at this point we're satisfied, and hey, let's look forward to the sunrise."

When the sun rose shortly thereafter, it was indeed breathtaking. In my more cerebral moments I always equated sunrise to rebirth, or the concept of new beginnings.... we have another chance to get it right. Whatever!

I saw Father Mike enjoying the sunrise as well. "Father, come on over and visit. Let me show you a sign I had to include in that little rock cairn... "Sure a little bit of heaven fell from the sky one day..."

"Lovely, Ed, and I do know the rest of the words to that little Irish ditty."

"I bet you do! What do you think of this spot, Father?"

"It is beautiful, Ed. I applaud the work you put in to get it done. You and Sidney Orenstein."

"That's right. Hey, I saw him around here before; he seems to have taken off."

At that moment, our friend appeared from behind the cabin. "Hello, Father, Edward. Wasn't that sunrise magnificent?"

"It surely was." Father Mike replied. "And it was no small effort on your part to carve out this wonderful little spot. You and Ed and a little help form the angels!"

Sidney walked over to me, took my arm and turned to Father Mike, and asked "Father, excuse us for a moment?"

"Certainly." He replied. "I need to be off to get myself prepared before the seven o'clock Mass."

Sidney and I walked over to a picnic table and sat down. Sidney was quite a bit older than I and had been a wonderful mentor to me from time to time, and was ungodly wealthy. I mean 'filthy rich'. His quiet and courtly manner exuded wisdom and confidence. He was well into his seventies, and as was his proper manner, always used my full name, Edward.

Sidney spoke first. "I couldn't help but notice Stan and his posse here before. It looked like they were laying in wait for someone."

I chuckled. "They were, Sidney. But I reminded them of the *10 O'clock News* last night, and the several interviews and statements that were made. Of course they claimed to be unaware of those announcements."

"Yes, I saw that and I was very pleased." acknowledged Sidney

"I know you were Sidney. That part of this puzzle seems to be solved, but you know, we could still have a murderer running around loose. And who's to say there aren't more targets?"

"No, Edward, Mr. Tydings was it, and whoever did it is done! My instinct tells me we have a murderer feeling a great sense of relief at revenge being satisfied. The attack was all about Mr. Horace Tydings. Granted I have no hard evidence to this fact, but these old bones tell me it is so. In fact I have always been a little surprised that there have not been more cases of physical attacks on our Mr. Tydings. You know very well that I knew Horace Tydings, and had various dealings with him. He had a good reputation of treating his partners fairly. It was his 'opponents", a sports metaphor he used, that he treated most maliciously and with utter disdain. He was not a very nice person. Polly and I never socialized with him, but, I always made money with him, I'll say that. It was the way he treated most people that disgusted me. I tell you, my instincts tell me the killer is probably someone Tydings damaged terribly and who is celebrating at this point about what happened. But I'm just one old man and at this point I am well away from the wars. Polly and I are so very happy here in Asheville and can't believe the time we spent in Miami, New York City and many European capitals chasing the almighty dollar. Not important now my friend; and Horace Tydings is gone and good riddance. I'll say this to you and you only, I think whoever was responsible for his death be given a measure of compassion. I know that's an awful thing to say, forgive me."

Not for the first time, I wondered who had ever really liked this guy Tydings.

"Come on, Edward; let me give you a ride home."

With that a green and grey Silver Cloud Rolls Royce pulled up, and the chauffer got out and had both back doors open before I could say, "Wow!"

"We have scaled back quite a bit since we moved here Edward, but some indulgences die hard. And I bet we can find a Macanudo in the humidor in the back seat."

"I'm in," I replied, "let's take the long way home." Thus I arrived in style, back to the inn in plenty of time to get things ready for the guests' breakfast.

Bill Oates was a little late but did show up for breakfast. He looked a bit sheepish, but I certainly knew how he felt, and kept my voice low. I made sure there continued to be plenty of ice water in his glass. Mary, as I expected, was just short of embarrassed.

The Greenlees had maps and brochures all around their places with wonderful eager looks on their faces. It was a new day, and they were off for more adventures. Phil and Barbara continued to fuss at each other. There was clearly some conflict there, and I thought they both seemed anxious to want a resolution but didn't know how to go about it. Something just wasn't right with them.

At that moment I remembered that I had committed to show up at the Little League game today. It was the first game for the *Polite Society* team. Chris and I agreed to sponsor a neighborhood team, which meant a fifty dollar entry fee to the general fund of the League and the cost of fifteen T-shirts and hats, emblazoned with *Polite Society's* logo. Big time!

I was really tired, but I committed in June to at least show up, and that's what I'd do. Then I'd come back and take a glorious nap.

Just then Chris reminded me, "You committed to show up for the first pitch at the Little League field at 10 o'clock."

"I know, I know. I was just thinking about that, and inasmuch as our appearance in the Club golf tournament has been cancelled, I can come home right away and take a delicious nap! There, I have my day already planned. I'm finished up here, honey, and I'm off! Let's hope our team wins, but I know I won't be around to see it. Be back soon."

Thus I was off to the ball field. It was to be a simple matter of meeting our team of kids, throwing out a ceremonial first ball, sticking around for a few obligatory innings, and then back for a nap before noon. I set off in a great frame of mind, without a clue as to what was really in store for me.

CHAPTER X

Little league….

Saturday, 10AM

As everyone in the immediate neighborhood knew, my favorite leisure spot is our front yard with my precious gardens and ever-present cigar. Our elevated property gave us a commanding view or vantage point to witness the comings and goings of folks in our little section of the historic district.

One day in the spring I had called down to Neil Washington as he walked by on his way to the corner bus stop. "Sure would be a great day for a baseball game."

Neil's face lit up, and he quickly asked "Can I come up and ask you a question?"

"Sure, young man, go around to the front gate and I'll meet you there."

Once inside Neil's head was on a swivel. "Gee, this is so nice. I never thought I would have the opportunity to be up here on this side of your fence. You really have a great spot to look down on people."

My eyebrows went up.

"Oh, I didn't mean it *that* way Mr. Loving; it just gives such a good overall view of the area."

"I know what you meant." I said with a little smile.

Neil was a young black man with a contagious energy and friendly personality. He was a nurse at Mission Hospital, and walked by each day on his way to the corner and the bus stop.

Totally disarmed, he asked, "Do you have any interest in kid's baseball?"

"I certainly do, Neil." Little did he know that I was an absolute romantic when it came to the game of baseball. He had no idea what a well of enthusiasm he tapped into.

From this casual beginning, we formed a first name friendship, based primarily on our mutual love of baseball. Neil, as I quickly learned was the coach and all around 'Mr. Everything' for our local Montford Little League team of kids up to age 13. I began to look out for him, and knowing his schedule, as work permitted, we would grab some time to sit on the side porch and cover all topics related to the game.

On another day on his way to the bus Neil yelled up to me as he walked by. "Hey, Ed, do you have a minute?"

"I sure do Neil, come on up."

"I saw in the paper today where you were recently inducted into the Citadel Athletic Hall of Fame for baseball."

'Yeah," I replied "They sure are scraping the bottom of the barrel now."

Neil looks startled, and then smiled broadly. "I'm sure not." he said. "Some time you can tell me all about it, and I know our kids will love it, to." He hesitated a minute, then continued.

"Ed, tell me if I'm being too forward, or not; would you and *Polite Society* be interested in sponsoring a Little League team?"

I hesitated for dramatic effect only; Neil had no way of knowing that I was thrilled to be asked.

"I guess we can do that, Neil, on one condition." Neil's grin disappeared.

"What condition?'

"You have to be involved, and be the coach. I want to sponsor your team." I said. Neil's grin reappeared.

"You know, Neil, when I was a kid and grew up in Brooklyn, there was a great deal of attention and financial resources given to sports activities."

Neil nodded, and wondered aloud; "It must have been nice not having to guess where the next dollar was coming from for balls, equipment, and the like."

"When we moved out to Long Island you would have thought you'd died and gone to heaven," I said, "if you saw the beautiful condition of the ball diamonds our children played on. Local businesses provided excellent support for nice, new, complete uniforms each year for every participating child. Many fields even had lighting for night time contests."

"Must be nice, must be very nice." responded Neil.

Now it's summer and here I am, in the midst of a horrendous weekend, driving to the ball field, ready to throw out the first ball, because of a commitment to the kids and particularly to my friend Neil Washington.

As I pulled up on the grass next to our Montford ball diamond the distance between North Shore Long Island and Montford, Asheville, couldn't be more pronounced.

Oh, the sounds and shouts were the same, the crack of a bat, the frantic shouts of enthusiastic young boys, and now girls too, were the same. But it was hard to miss the weeds encroaching on the infield, the long grass in the outfield and the somewhat crooked chalked baselines and outfield lines of our local field. There were noticeably deep holes on either side of home plate from much prior usage and I saw that the pitcher's mound was relatively flat, and the 'rubber' was chewed up old wood.

But the game of baseball crossed all social, ethnic and financial lines. It was universal. The condition of the field didn't matter. The tee shirts as opposed to full uniforms didn't matter; the presence of well worn sneakers rather than cleats didn't matter. Hats a size or two too large or too small, as were some of the tee shirts didn't matter. The game, whether in Yankee Stadium, some poorly lit minor league ball field or some out-post sand lot in Asheville, North Carolina, was still *the game*. It was pitcher versus batter, it was encouraging chatter from both sides, it was little fists pounding into leather gloves, and it was truly a beautiful scene.

"What are you doing here?" shouted Neil. He came running over, and really looked quite surprised. "Boy, I really didn't think you would show, and I wouldn't blame you if you hadn't."

"Oh, it's only for a few minutes," I said, "and I did give you my promise."

"You're quite a guy Ed. I was just explaining to the team that you might not show. What happened on Thursday is the talk of the neighborhood, big news! I know the kids will be impressed with your presence. Come; let's give them their pre-game talk."

We all assembled in the outfield; Neil went over signals, the opening line up, and the fact that this was always to be considered just a game, a clearly treasured pastime, but that everyone was included and everyone would play. I was introduced and I shook hands with each player, and didn't you know it, we had a young girl who preferred to think of herself as the starting second baseman. I loved it!

The umpire was calling everyone in. I managed to deliver the ceremonial first ball, on a fly to the catcher, and then the symbolic call by the umpire of "Play Ball!"

I was soon wrapped up in the game, and was shouting encouragement, instructions, and a little derision for the opposing team. Forget the nap; we had a ball game to win! In some ways, this was just what the doctor ordered. It was a wonderful tonic, a great escape from the events of the last few days.

'Sandlot baseball'. Just the term itself conjured up for most American men a time of innocence and fair play. Your best pitcher against their best batter. The chatter began: "Bet you can't hit this." "Swing batter, swing batter." "Bet you can't catch this." What fun; blue skies, bright sun, green grass. I admitted the purist in me still hadn't embraced the sound of an aluminum bat hitting a baseball.

I was the recipient of a few stares; like: 'what are you doing here?' Balanced against these were more nods of 'welcome and acceptance for helping our kids.' These were good, honest, hard working parents and social barriers have no place in the enjoyment of youth athletic activities.

I was reminded again of the painful, and not easy, gentrification process underway in Montford. At the turn of the twentieth century this area had been the grand neighborhood for the local pooh-bahs. Not so, now. So many of the wonderful old Colonial, Victorian and Arts and Crafts houses which line the main drag, Montford Avenue, had been turned into low income apartments. They were now being restored, little by little to their former grandeur, by new people with new money.

Oh well, it surely wasn't something I wanted to resolve at this point. Back to the game and some enjoyment for a change. Our kids were good; Neil has done a great job of coaching, and keeping them focused.

About this time I noticed a young man coming my way, behind the backstop. I couldn't say why, really, but my first impression was that he really didn't belong here. As he got closer I became more convinced he was out or place.

"Ed Loving?"

"Yes?"

He did not extend his hand nor did he look particularly friendly.

"I'm Larry Tydings."

The spell was broken. Just looking at this young man brought the angst of the previous few days flooding back. The quizzical look on my face indicated that I couldn't quite place him.

"I'm Horace Tydings son, and I've come to this God-forsaken little town to find out what happened to my father. He called me two days ago on his cell phone and we got disconnected. I tried him back but got no response. Then later that afternoon, a real shocker, our headquarters hears from the local police here that my father is dead under what appears to be suspicious circumstances. Subsequently your lovely local media can't contain itself from proclaiming that you were the number one suspect."

"Hold on!" I sensed something significant barely glossed over. "Tell me again, what time did he call?"

"As if you're really interested. He called me at 9:45 Thursday morning. I know because I instinctively looked at my watch after seeing on caller ID that it was my father, because I had a meeting at 11.

"Are you sure that it was actually your father, Horace Tydings, on the call?"

"Of course I'm sure! I know my own father. He asked me if I was prepared for the meeting, because I only had an hour; and he called me 'laddie', a name that only he used, and usually in private. He told me that he was here, in Asheville, at your bed and breakfast, and things weren't going as he wanted. Then the call dropped and nothing. When I tried to call back his phone went to voicemail. Just like him."

Young Tydings took a deep breath, but it was not a calming one. My question had diverted his attention but now he was back on track as the avenger. He gave me a belligerent stare and went angrily on. "I guarantee you that I'll get to the bottom of this. I have a team of attorneys on call, and our own private investigators who should be here today, by late afternoon. When I called at your inn, your wife told me I could find you here. Just great, the killer's at a ball game."

Oh boy! I thought. Thanks a lot Chris! But I guessed it was better to somehow contain this loose cannon, rather than let him stir things up all over town. I looked around and saw some questioning stares.

"Let's get away from these people who are sitting here enjoying the game. Let's take a walk over there by my car in the parking lot."

"You can't order me around. I'll talk to you any place I like."

I figured that if I moved away anyway, he'd have to follow me to continue his little tirade. This proved correct. We got away from most of the folks, and stood among the parked cars.

"You have a lot of explaining to do, Mr. Ed Loving." The sarcasm and his intense dislike for me was quite evident. I tried to think quickly whether I had ever said or done anything to this little squirt.

I offered "What you really want to do, with your team of attorneys, is to make a visit as soon as possible downtown to see our District Attorney. Next on your visit list, again, particularly for your private investigators, is to visit our Chief of Detectives. Both of these men are deeply involved in the investigation of your father's death, and I believe they would be highly disturbed about you simply going around town on your own, and badgering people.

Larry Tydings didn't look happy. "There you go again, giving me orders."

I knew now that I never had any dealings with this guy and I didn't expect that any one ever could have any meaningful dealings with him. The old man always found a way to install him as an officer in newly acquired companies, for no other reason than to provide him with a salary. He never was placed in any position of responsibility. I almost felt sorry for him. His meal ticket was gone, and I was sure he knew that there were many people who would love to eliminate his company positions. He probably was alone now, without friends, allies or anyone for that matter unless he was willing to pay dearly for support. Pretty sad.

At this point another car pulled into the lot and parked right up next to us; Lieutenant Richard Davis had arrived, like the cavalry, to the rescue. He got out of his car, came up to me and with a big smile inquired, "Well, did you see the news last night? Are you happy now?"

Without even acknowledging Tydings, he further explained how he had gone by the inn to get my reaction and Chris told him I would be delighted to see him here at the ballgame.

This time I gratefully said to myself, "Thanks, Chris!"

My friend Richard turned his attention to Mr. Larry Tydings.

"You've been a busy boy my young friend."

"I'm not your friend," barked young Tydings. "And don't treat me like some youngster."

Lieutenant Davis went on, seemingly not having heard a word:

"I have gotten a string of calls about your unannounced visits all over town; Mission Hospital, the *Citizen Times,* our local TV station Channel 13, and the Mayor's office. If I was of a mind, I'm sure I could make a case for severe harassment against you, young fellow. You were uniformly arrogant, obnoxious and abusive at each stop you made. And I am now here to demand that you cease and desist or I will lock you up in our little God-forsaken jail. Have I made myself clear?"

Larry Tydings mumbles something unintelligible in an effort to hold onto some measure of his dignity, and he snarled through clenched teeth: "My attorneys and I will meet with you later today, Lieutenant Davis."

"Of course." Lieutenant Davis hastened to add: "Remember, my boy, my office isn't very big, so don't bring too many folks with you."

Tydings looks at both of us, sensed correctly that the meeting was concluded, and stalked off to his rental car and drove off. It was compact car. Indeed, I thought to myself, this boy is already confronting what life was to be 'post Daddy'!

"You enjoyed that didn't you Lieutenant?"

"Yes, I did," laughed the Lieutenant. "If there's one thing I can't stand, it's wise guys from Miami, who think they know it all, and have no respect for our small town ways."

"I hear you, Lieutenant, loud and clear."

At this point, Neil Washington strolled over.

"Well, I know you didn't see all of it, but the game's over and we won, Hi, Lieutenant, glad to see you out at the ball park. You had the kids nervous for a moment, but they saw you smiling at Ed here, and figured everything was cool!"

Lieutenant Davis replied, "Everything is cool, Neil, just as you and the kids say."

The detective continued, "See, Ed, Neil here is what neighborhood involvement is all about. You are so good for the kids, Neil. They really listen to you, and look up to you. I wish we had more people willing to get involved in the neighborhood with our kids."

We all exchange looks. I say: "I hear you, Lieutenant." We all had a good laugh, and headed off in different directions. I was hopeful that this trio would get together again, sooner than later. The neighborhood did need us.

I almost forgot something. "Hey, Lieutenant? Can you come by the inn this afternoon? I'd like to go over some information I've developed."

Already in his car, Davis looked at me with a half smile. "You haven't been up to your own investigations have you?"

"Me?" I declared. "Nah, I just want to sort a few things out with you."

"Okay, Ed. I'll see you around three o'clock".

CHAPTER XI

Gathering information....

Saturday 12:30 PM

"Honey I'm home." I said as I breezed into the cottage. No one's here. Chris must still be at the inn. I went over and found her in the kitchen preparing Griddled Cheesecakes for tomorrow's breakfast. She'd prepared the raspberry sauce. I saw she kept a few berries aside for me. Now she was busy measuring out the cheeses that would go into this tasty treat for our guests in the morning.

"I'm back, I'm tired, and oh yeah, thanks a bunch for sending Larry Tydings down to the ball field, but then again I do thank you for sending Lieutenant Davis after him."

"I thought you'd appreciate that." said Chris. "Tydings just walked right in through the front door about 11 o'clock or so, and was really rather abusive and rude. He told me he had a suite at the Grove Park Inn, as he was 'understandably' unwilling to go near any of the local bed and breakfasts. We were in his words not up to the 'Tydings standard'. I really wanted him just to go. I didn't feel very comfortable around him, as I was by myself in the empty house. I told him where you were as much to get rid of him as to comply with his demand of your whereabouts and I provided directions. Since you said you weren't staying for the game, I'd hoped you'd be on your way home before he got there."

"Well, he found me, dear heart, and interrupted the game for me! Apart from all the nonsense, I have to tell you how much I enjoyed watching the kids play. There weren't nearly as many parents there as we used to see at Charles' and Everett's games on Long Island. There were enough adult coaches in the bleachers though. Neil Washington, bless his heart, really works hard with the players. There is, I might point out, an outstanding second baseman, a cute, little tow head with long braids! A girl! It's a brave new world!"

"Right after I sent young Mr. Tydings on his way, Lieutenant Davis came by here looking for him; something about his stirring up everyone down at City Hall and at the newspaper. He'd just missed Tydings by a few minutes."

Chris looked a little guilty as she explained this.

"Forget it, honey," I said. "I was relieved to see Lieutenant Davis. Young Tydings had me cornered in the parking lot and was acting quite irrationally. Davis arrived under a full head of steam and told young Tydings in no uncertain terms to cool it, and that they should plan to meet on an official basis in the DA's office down town late this afternoon. 'Our Richard' told Tydings that it would be appropriate to have his attorney with him. I believe that I'm out of it now, and I have no reason to have any further contact with young Tydings."

"Chris, I must be getting a little soft. Believe it or not, in spite of his obnoxious and in-my-face actions by young Mr. Tydings, I can't help but feel a little sorry for him. He is now, in all probability completely on his own. I'm guessing it's for the first time in his life, and certainly with out much of a favorably disposed constituency among the various company executives. I'll bet there'll be a goodly amount of pay-back coming to this young man from them."

"Although I have to agree with you, this is just another side-show that we really don't need. But you're right. The poor guy is going to be out in the cold, and I'm sure he's ill prepared for what will confront him."

I glanced at the clock on the kitchen wall. "Look at the time, almost two o'clock, and I still haven't had my nap. I'm exhausted."

Just then our friends Ellen and Jerry from the inn across the street walked up the back steps and into the kitchen. Jerry greeted us with a hearty "Hello, hello you dear people. Can we buy you lunch up at the club?"

"Is there anything we can help you with?" asked Ellen. "You two must be wrecks! Imagine a dead body one day and a stupid ill-advised, and as it turns out, a totally incorrect news article the next day, not to mention our little miss bitch puss on Channel 10."

It was obvious that Ellen, bless her heart, was really steamed.

"Ellen, you dear girl, don't be shy! Please tell us what you really think of all this. Give us your real opinion!"

Ellen's visits had a wonderful way of putting Chris in a sunny mood. Ellen laughed and continued.

"Chris, I want to do something. Now, mind you, I don't want to meddle, or get in your way, but I want to stand up and strike back at these fools. Can you imagine?"

"I did see a rather lame retraction in the paper this morning," said Jerry. "What's that all about?"

"Jerry, did you all see the local 10 o'clock news last night?" I asked.

Ellen answered for him. "No, we didn't. We were playing bridge late with the Wilson's. I wish we had been playing with you. That couple is just like a sit-com. They were constantly at each other's throats during the game. It makes me forget what I'm doing as I follow their chattering. Any way!"

Chris outlined for Ellen and Jerry the gist of the news conferences as well as Lieutenant Davis' report on the actions of the editor, and the TV station's manager.

"Great! That's good news," sang Ellen, "now we can all get back to normal. I hope all of the other bed and breakfast owners, and Ed, your good friends at the Chamber of Commerce are up to date, too."

"Yeah," chimed in Jerry true to form. "Hell, if you knew this last night, you could have called me and we could have still played in the tournament. Geeze!"

" Jerry, Ellen, listen to me. The fact still remains that there is a murderer out there who has not been identified. Aside from the very nice things said about me by the DA and Davis, the murderer could be anyone. Who knows, maybe he could strike again."

"Ed, you don't believe that." Ellen was annoyed now.

"You're just trying so scare us."

Chris jumped in. "Hold on everyone. This apparent homicide is still unsolved, but I have a good feeling about Lieutenant Davis and his people. I think they will be resolving this soon. I must admit that

I didn't have a high regard for him prior to this; in fact I was probably most influenced by his appearance, and how he conducted himself around the neighborhood. I have certainly seen a different side of him during this investigation, and I have to say, I like what I've seen."

"Wow, Chris", said Jerry, "this; about the same guy whose close friends refer to us as 'THE B&B PEOPLE'! This whole mess has made for some strange bed-fellows' – no pun intended."

I took Jerry off to the side and recounted my early morning pow-wow up on Spring Point. At the same time that he seemed pleased that I was able to zing our Chamber president, he expressed a disappointment that he had not been called to go. That was my friend Jerry.

Turning back to Chris and Ellen I addressed Jerry's initial invitation. "Okay guys, we appreciate the concern and kind words and the late lunch invitation, but I have been up since four o'clock this morning. I am beat, and I need a nice nap. Let's plan on a dinner at the club next Wednesday. Jerry you and I can tee off about three o'clock, and still get back in time for a nice casual dinner with the ladies downstairs at the Pub. How about it?"

Again, Ellen answered for Jerry.

"Fine with us. Chris, maybe you and I can do a little personal shopping that day before dinner. We'll check out any Stein Mart sales!"

I groaned inwardly. Ellen's 'personal shopping' and 'bargain hunting' could put Chris into the American Express Hall of Fame if she lost her caution, and followed Ellen's lead.

Ellen continued: "Oh, Chris, I'm so glad you both are hanging in there. In fact, you're doing better than I would have thought, certainly better than I think we would have. We've gotten several calls from folks who naturally want to know what's going on, you know, looking for a little inside info. You should feel very satisfied at the amount of good will for you from all these local folks. Of course I'm not surprised, but at least I can now give these people a really positive spin."

"Ellen, you are a dear. And Jerry, you take good care of my best girlfriend!" Chris had a sincere smile, and a little catch in her voice as she walked them to door.

As our friends headed out across the parking area Chris said, "You have a ton of messages downstairs. Your personal phone line has been ringing off the hook since this morning. I suggest you check the calls for any emergency before you head off to the land of Nod.

"Honey, I'm going downstairs to do just that. I've got some serious thinking to do, too. A good Cohiba shouldn't interfere with that process. Lieutenant Davis, or I should say our good friend Richard, is coming by later and I hope I can get him to compare notes with me. What do you think?"

"I think," She replied, "that you should remember his explicit instruction that we leave the homicide investigation to him and his professional associates."

"I do, Chris, but come on; you really didn't think I could let this go and sit idly by. No way! It all means just too much to us. I've been on the phone with several people, as you must have guessed, what with me running down to the office every free moment."

Oh well, Chris seemed resigned to my pleadings, and with a rueful smile and a deep diva-like sigh, exclaimed, "Go get 'em, tiger!"

As I entered my office I could see the message light blinking furiously. There were nine messages according to the little display window. Probably a lot of people just wanting to know what was going on, I thought. As I guessed, there were four calls from concerned local friends waiting to be updated. However, five of the messages were from folks in Miami and Orlando that I had reached out to in the last two days. I was pleasantly surprised at the turn around time, and I hoped these return calls were fruitful.

A good cigar later, it was three-thirty, and with the calls returned I had time to reflect on what I had found out, and perhaps what I still didn't know. Some of my guesses could prove correct, while some were probably off the mark. At any rate, I narrowed down certain possibilities, and my dilemma was what, or how much, or even should I, share my information with Lieutenant Davis. The plain fact was that I had less than hard and fast evidence. All I had was speculation, and certain select information that could conveniently be used to support my conclusions. Not what you could call praise worthy investigative techniques. I knew I had some truly helpful information, but until I used it to support some good old fashioned facts, I guess it'd be better to keep it all to myself.

I'd better write some of this down; I wanted to make sure I recollected my conversations accurately while they are still fresh in my mind. Too bad I didn't actually record the conversations.

I knew that Lieutenant Davis was hard at work with many more resources than I had, that's for sure. Perhaps all I was doing was duplicating his efforts. I wondered if I should ask him about it. And yet, it was still vivid in my mind how I'd promised to stay out of the way and let the professionals do their jobs. On the other hand, all I was doing really was supplementing his efforts. I wasn't getting in his way. I didn't see that whatever calls I'd made, and information I'd acquired would in any way compromise his efforts. On the contrary, he'd no doubt find my information quite helpful! Talk about 'spin city', I could go to work in Washington.

At that moment, the phone rang and as I picked it up I could hear a little click. Chris was on the extension. She had the only extension for this line on her console in the kitchen.

"Ed, this is Lieutenant Davis. I'd like to come by to chat with you about the progress of our investigation." Not "Richard". He must be calling from his office.

"Of course, Lieutenant." I said.

The only response from the Lieutenant was the sound of him hanging up.

Several thoughts welled up at the same time. Was he taking me in as a conspiratorial partner? Did he have new doubts regarding my story of the events upon discovering Tydings body? Did he want to talk about my conversations with young Mr. Tydings? Was I in for a dressing down?

After I hung up, I heard Chris on the stairs. I was not sure I could read the expression on her face.

"I'm sure you heard me pick up when you answered that last call." I agreed that I had.

"What is up with Lieutenant Davis? I hope you haven't been sticking your nose in unwelcome places. I hope he's not coming over here to chew you out. You know we both gave him our word that we would not go off on our own, and complicate his life with our amateurish investigation. We gave our word that we would leave it to the professionals. You do remember that?"

"Yes, I certainly do!" I respond with a good deal of sincerity that I did not feel. The girl knows! And she was giving me that "I hear you, but I don't believe you" look.

"At any rate," I blustered on, "what could be the harm in my doing a little calling around anyway?" I could pretend a goodly degree of indignation when I felt I had to.

Chris was not to be denied. "Don't pull that phony sense of indignation with me. You call someone, they call someone, they feel a little pressure, boom, boom, boom, and when Davis or his people call, someone decides to clam up! Or something like that! I don't even want to know who you called or what you've said.

"I agree; wholeheartedly. You know me."

"Yes, I do know you," she replied. On that Chris turned her back on me and climbed back up the stairs.

Whew, that left a bit of a chill in the air. I'd better gather my wits here. What I needed was that nap. I'll just shut my eyes right here and wait for Davis. Nice comfortable chair and a nice quiet office, nice.......

Don't anyone forget;: this is my house, my business, my life! Why shouldn't I be interested in seeing this cleared up? If not me, then who then has a greater motivation for clearing up this mess? Truth be told, and I would never say this aloud, or share it with anyone, particularly Chris; who did the world a favor?

I'm so sleepy; I can barely keep my head up.

Suddenly I jerked my head up. How could I have been so dense? Of course, that was probably what happened. Let me get Lieutenant Davis on the phone right away.

" Richard...Ed here. I want to share some thoughts with you. I know you'll be interested. How soon can we get together to discuss things? Can you be here earlier than you thought today?"

"Sure," replied Lieutenant Davis. "I'm on my way if that's all right."

"Come right ahead," I said. "I'm kind of anxious to go over this with you.

Shortly thereafter: "But where's the evidence, Ed?" Lieutenant Davis was being a little picky about this. I was becoming surer in my own mind of the prime suspect. Why wasn't the Lieutenant convinced?

"We need hard evidence, Ed, before we can proceed. I appreciate your input here, but I need more than your convictions about who is guilty. 'Where's the beef', comes to mind."

Oh, great, now he's a regular comedian, I thought. Why was this so difficult to get across to him? I felt like I was wading around in molasses. This shouldn't be this hard. I needed a brilliant idea here, and I just couldn't grasp it. It was floating around out there just out of my reach. Everything seemed to be in slow motion, just kind of drifting by....

"Ed, Ed, can you hear me?"

That was Chris at the top of the stairs shouting down to me. "Can you hear me?"

I was at best a little groggy, and looked around to get a feel for the familiar surroundings. Suddenly it dawned on me: I must have dozed off here in my chair, and dreamed...What was the dream?

"Ed, dear, Lieutenant Davis pulled into the parking area. Finish up down there and come on up."

Hmmm! I guess I was dreaming. Let me see if I can remember. Where are my notes? "Be right there, honey."

The stress of the last few days has finally gotten to me. Let's hope Davis had some good news, and then maybe he'd listen to my hunches. I hoped he'd be willing to listen to me. Of course, I already knew what he was going to say: I had no real evidence.

CHAPTER XII

Comparing notes….

Saturday, mid-afternoon

It was time for me to determine a game plan, or better yet to systematically put together my many conversations over the last day and a half. It was time "to use the little grey cells." My suspicions were becoming stronger that Tydings just may have been struck down intentionally by the hand of another one of our guests. I had to uncover the facts. Surely, Lieutenant Davis would understand, and even appreciate this.

There was no doubt that many folks had been mistreated and suffered at the hands of Tydings, and likewise many people would have ample cause to see him suffer as well. Yet, it remained a great argument that someone here at the inn was responsible. One who could move about quite easily without much attention paid, and who was aware of the daily schedules and rituals of most folks in the inn.

It appeared that no one, other than his obnoxious son, was sad to hear of Tydings passing. To a great extent, it was just the opposite. Could a case be made that justice truly had been done? Was it proper to blatantly celebrate the fact? The answer quite honestly was an unqualified no! In our justice system and even in our military in times of armed conflict, one must act with compassion for the guilty or the fallen foe. Somewhere, each one of us deserves to have someone mourn. This somewhat callous attitude toward Tydings demise had become just a little unsettling. Now, sitting at my desk, prime cigar in hand, it was time to consider my next moves. Right then there was a voice at the top of the stairs.

"Ed, are you there?"

"Come on down, Lieutenant, I was hoping you could make it. Come on down, make yourself comfortable. Here, can I offer you a real cigar?"

"Please, Ed, I know my little cigarillos are quite offensive and deathly sweet smelling, but it's all I can afford. You know, we're all driven by the costs of our vices."

"When this is all over Lieutenant, I want you to come by on a regular basis, and we can just sit on my side porch, light up a good cigar, and pass the time more pleasantly than now. Promise me you'll consider it."

"I will Ed, if you'll have me!"

"Good." "Now, Lieutenant", I started.

"Please, Ed, before you go any further, do call me Richard."

Oh yeah, we were alone. I just didn't feel that now was the appropriate time to start a first name basis. But perhaps in the friendly confines of my den I could do it. All right, Richard it is.

"Richard, you didn't really believe that I would sit idly by during this time, and not get involved somehow. Did you really think so?"

Richard looked at me with a bemused grin and with an almost inaudible laugh admitted, "No I didn't… not really. I guess you're entitled, Ed, and being around you now for the past three days, I must say I would be very surprised if you hadn't done some of your own probing. Hell, your inn's reputation is at stake here. Also, you've been kicked around pretty good by the local newspaper and TV station, not to mention your 'good friends' at the Chamber of Commerce." Richard had to chuckle at this. Then he continued.

"I'm sure that some of your fellow inn-keepers are none too happy themselves with the last few days. I think you've held up quite well frankly, and I applaud you for how you've handled everything."

"Alright, Richard, tell me about your theories on this case. Maybe they'll help me solidify my own thoughts."

"Well, as far as your guests go, they all seem to have unshakable alibis that revolve around being a good distance from the inn when Tydings took his fall into the pond and died. Time of death, at least according to the coroner's report seems to be quite close to your original 911 call at Thursday morning. When I met with you folks Thursday night after wine and cheese, they all quickly supplied enough information to establish their whereabouts that morning. The Oates were in the middle of a horse back riding class at the Biltmore Estate and had ample witnesses to confirm this."

"The Greenlees had a Biltmore Estate Entrance ticket and Visa receipt, dated and stamped Thursday at 10:15 AM and lastly. The Kerrys had a Visa receipt with his signature from a Biltmore Village gas station dated Thursday at 9:58 AM. This would appear to rule out your guests. It would be physically impossible to get to the inn from where they all were at the narrow time frame for Tydings death. Being satisfied with these alibis was our initial objective. But, I'm having them carefully checked out, and then rechecked.

The Lieutenant continued. "Preliminary coroner's results are in and reveal the possibility of blunt force trauma to the head as the cause of death, and that may explain the ugly bruise on Tydings face. Also there was no water in his lungs. The bruise, according to the MD doing the coroner's report, would be inconsistent with simply falling half way head first into the pond. Add to this the unlikely ability for anyone to escape the property without you seeing or hearing them further complicates the picture. The idea of a simple random act of violence becomes further unlikely, as does a robbery based on the jewelry remaining on the body along with Tydings wallet with an unusual amount of cash still in it."

"So" I blurted out, "what you're saying is that you have nothing! Am I right?" I immediately saw that this was the wrong approach. We were going to get nowhere if Davis crawled into a defensive mode. He didn't answer me; simply gave me something like the old 'fish-eye'. I hurried to make amends. "Okay, okay, forget if you will what I just said. Your four prime suspects, including me, have passed muster, and now you're telling me that the universe of suspects has grown exponentially."

I continued: "Let me tell you what I've done and observed since finding Tydings on Thursday morning. I appreciate all that you and your associates have already done, and before we go any further; remember I had the considerable advantage of knowing and talking with several people in South Florida and elsewhere. And of course, I have been right here at the scene and have been able at least to observe our guests. I have some strong suspicions about what might have happened here although admittedly, I am lacking for the fine details. Proof of my gut feelings or hunches might be very difficult to obtain. It would more likely have to be a confession!"

Davis had regained some of his gravitas and asserted himself. "Alright big boy, tell me what you've done, and what you're thinking."

"First, you must understand, Richard, that I did nothing that would interfere with you or your professional law enforcement associates. I made several calls to businessmen, former bank associates, attorney friends and selected other resources around the country, but mostly in the state of Florida."

"I observed the present guests in the inn, starting off as you did treating them as prime suspects. I have a keen eye for human behavior, developed over many years – from the school yards of Brooklyn through college at the Citadel, my military years and especially during my corporate lending and management years. Yet as I said, I see no way to prove my suspicions."

"The Greenlees, John and Sherry are a young couple from Winston-Salem and totally unaware of Horace Tydings and his activities. When originally questioned they were determined to stay the weekend even when I offered them a 'rain check' due to the unforeseen events. I'm afraid I became convinced rather early on that this youthful and energetic couple was simply not up to murder, and observing their actions since has pretty much convinced me of their innocence."

"The Oates couple is next. Bill and Mary have a history with Horace Tydings. Bill has quite openly admitted this, and was bald-faced honest in his true feelings of justice being done in the demise of Horace Tydings. Bill lost his Chief Financial Officer position because of Tydings, and as he explained, possibly his mother as the result of his father's firing and lack of getting his full pension. On the surface these seemed to me excellent motives for Bill Oates. Yet, in speaking with several resources in the Gainesville area, I was told Bill's dad was not a very good sales manager, and his position as sales manager was tenuous at best, even before Tydings took over the company. In fact, if the old man had had the good sense to save a few bucks he would have been able to obtain adequate medical care for his wife.

"Slow down, slow down, and let me get this in my book." Richard pleaded.

I continued, a bit slower. "Behind the scenes, young Bill was well aware of this, and knew quite well the inadequacies and lack of personal assets and savings of his dad. In fact, I was told the son did what he could money-wise for his folks. Bill's reputation is outstanding across the board from several business folks in Gainesville. He could easily locate with good solid companies, but has elected to go slowly in the process, not wanting to get burned again. It was volunteered that while the story and events of dismissal were true, it probably was the best thing – long term- that could have happened to him. My observations of Bill and his wife over the last two days have been quite positive, and in my opinion he was not involved, nor should he be a suspect in this tragic event."

The good Lieutenant continued furiously writing all this down in short hand in his notebook. When he finished his last jotting, he looked up and said, "And that leaves Phil Kerry."

"Yes Richard, that leaves Phil Kerry. I'll go much slower now. Again, Richard, I was able to speak to several people who knew both the Kerry family and Phil in particular. He was described as a very sensitive, introspective young man and quite talented in the home decor fashions field. It seemed his family, his father, had an old and well respected furniture chain in Florida, headquartered in Melbourne. There were five stores. It was four years ago. You guessed it; here we go with the 'small world' again. At that time the local state economy had been in a downturn so predictable in Florida. Things were coming back, but many companies including Mr. Kerry's had used up their cash reserves. Banks weren't ready to lend yet. Tydings and his cronies became aware of this particular situation and agreed to buttress the companies flagging fortunes for a major interest in the business."

"This all sounds so familiar; and so predictable," said Richard.

"Kerry senior was no match for Tydings and his clever legal minions. The acquisition documents clearly stated, beneath whole layers of wherefores and whereases, what remedies could be pursued by the majority partner based on the business' inability to meet its obligations in a timely fashion. Needless to say, continued losses by the company triggered actions for Tydings to achieve total asset control for his cash infusion. Again, Kerry senior continued to think that as had happened before during a stagnant economy, all would work its way out, and when the business was solidly back on its feet, he could convince Tydings to accept a buy back from him. Ah, but here we get a concrete case in point of the late Mr. Horace Tydings. It seems the underlying land on which the main store, warehouse and headquarters were located was really the desired company assets for Tydings and his associates. He never had any interest in the intrinsic nature of the businesses he bought versus their cash value. So, Richard you can guess what happened next!"

"I know, Ed. By this time even this less than sophisticated, small town cop can probably finish the story."

I went on. "The furniture business was wound down, the inventory auctioned off for less than cost, the employees were dismissed, and old man Kerry was unceremoniously discarded as well. And guess what? Tydings made a an absolute bundle on selling the land! Old man Kerry was a broken man. I'll spare you any more grim details – he unfortunately solved his problems by taking his own life. The younger Kerry, our guest Phil, proceeded to deal poorly with the situation. He apparently expended what little savings he had to pursue Tydings in court, among trying to prove the complete deception of Tydings investment. End result: the transaction was iron clad in Tydings favor as only high priced legal muscle can provide."

"There you have it Richard, another family dramatically and horrifically affected by our esteemed and very dead guest, Horace Tydings."

Richard listened with an ever deepening frown creasing his brow. "All of this is fine Ed. No I don't mean it that way. What I really mean is so you have a strong motive here, no doubt; but what's the upshot here. Did Phil Kerry do it? And how do you explain his physical presence elsewhere at the stated time of death, at some distance from the inn?"

"I don't know! My sources are impeccable and I just have a gut feeling about this. I told you before, proof for what I'm proposing will be very difficult to obtain. What I'm counting on is, if the proper setting can be developed, a confession will come. Richard, here's what I'd like to do, and I would like your consent to go ahead with my plan."

I proceeded to lay out my strategy to Richard and ended up by saying "God help us that we can resolve this dilemma in a controlled and reasonable manner."

CHAPTER XIII

Confession is good for the soul....

Saturday 4:30 PM

All of the guests were back and in their rooms freshening up and preparing for their final wine and cheese get together. The threat of, and surprisingly enough the forecast, for late afternoon showers had clearly influenced an early return from their day's activities. The dark gray overcast skies called for just about every light in the inn to be on.

The time had come.

As I ascended the stairs, I knew Lieutenant Davis was in the library, ready and available if I had to call on him. I approached the guest's door and gently knocked.

"Who's there?" came a soft muted voice.

"It's Ed. May I come in?"

Barbara Kerry slowly opened the door and stepped aside for me to enter. An air of resignation was clearly apparent, and by all appearances she had been crying. Phil lay on the bed, one arm across his eyes; seemingly to block out the harsh realities of events around him.

"We've actually been waiting for this visit," said Barbara, as she moved to the corner of the room.

"I want to talk to you, and I want you to listen very carefully." I took a seat at the desk as Phil sat up reluctantly; but he gave every indication that he was prepared to listen to me.

"Let me tell you how I think this all went down."

There was no reason to dance around what "this" meant; nor was it necessary for a long analytical preamble. I was sure Phil and Barbara had discussed "it" repeatedly over the last forty-eight hours and there now appeared on both their faces a certain resignation. If I had to guess, they were relieved to be able to discuss "it" openly with someone else. The last two days must have been hell for them because deep down these were good people. I suspected, now, more than ever, that this was all a very unfortunate happening.

I looked directly at young Kerry.

"Here's how I think things happened, Phil, and please hear me out. After breakfast, on your way to the parking lot you spotted Tydings sitting by the koi pond. You told Barbara to go to the car that you would be along in a minute. You then approached Tydings who, at first more than likely, didn't even recognize you. You introduced yourself. I can't say for sure what words were exchanged, but no doubt you were enraged by well known prior events. You, as a good and loyal son, loved and respected your dad. And here, right before you was the man –evil incarnate- who ruined your family as well as your business career. Am I right so far?"

Phil looked down, and mumbled, almost inaudibly, "Go on."

"I don't know how long or how much went on between you, but my guess is very simply, that you slugged him, and then you ran off to the parking lot, and proceeded on to your planned day with Barbara."

"Phil, can you now fill in the blanks for me. Lieutenant Davis and I are of a mind that while this was a tragic death, it was certainly not pre-meditated. Rather it was a momentary act of rage gone horribly wrong."

"Tell him," begged Barbara as she approached Phil. "We must get beyond this somehow. It can't go on any more. Please. "

Phil sat up straighter, without a bit of calculation or guile on his face, and started to speak.

"You have most of it right, Ed, and I appreciate your support and understanding. Also Barbara is right. We must get beyond this, and face the consequences. The last two days have been an utter nightmare."

I hoped my rather deep sigh went undetected, and I sat ready to hear Phil's explanation of what happened between him and Horace Tydings at the koi pond. Here was to be that story that Richard had alluded to yesterday. Would we in fact buy into it, and support it or not?

"You have to believe me, Ed; we did not choose your inn for our holiday because we knew that Tydings would be here. Quite honestly,

I would go out of my way to stay away from him at all costs. I heard him enter late Wednesday night, noisy and condescending. I knew that no good was to come of this. I was so relieved that Tydings did not come down for breakfast – or that might have developed into an ugly situation. A little later, on our way out around 9:30 I did see him sitting by the pond. I asked Barbara to go and get in the car; that I just had to have a few words with the guest by the pond. She was completely unaware of who was there or my intent."

Phil continued haltingly: "I approached that bastard, and asked him if he knew who I was. He expressed no apparent recognition of me, and indicated that he could care less. 'Beat it! Leave me alone, kid.' was all he said. I fought to stay calm and under control and proceeded to identify myself, at which he did show some slight recognition. 'Beat it, kid, leave me alone' he repeated and with a sneer added that he didn't have any time for my 'sad story'. He laughed at me. He asked if I'd saved enough money to take him to court again. He wanted to know if I liked getting beaten in court. At that point I lost it, Ed. He realized that I was angry, whereupon he jumped up at me. With a mean scowl he stepped menacingly toward me. I did take a swing at him and caught him high on the cheek. I might have cut him with my school ring. To his credit he didn't go down; he simply back pedaled some. He was mad though....and at that second I knew that at least I had gotten his attention...small victory. I came to my senses, appalled at what I had done. I'm not a violent man. He called me a few choice names, asked if I were 'happy now', and said it was his turn to take me to court now, and he'd win again. He laughed, low and nasty."

"I left him there, muttering to himself and joined Barbara in the parking lot and we went on our way to the Biltmore Estate. When I left him, he was very much alive, pawing at his cheek with his big beefy hand. I have no godly idea what happened after that."

By this time Phil was on the edge of the bed with a 'please believe me' look of contrition on his face.

"You just have to believe me; Ed. Tydings was very much alive when I left him."

Phil and Barbara sat together, holding hands, looking sad and dispirited. Phil indeed looked relieved to finally get this off his conscience. Confession is indeed good for the soul.

"Now what?" asked Phil.

"I honestly don't know." I replied. "You will have to be questioned by the police first, and Phil, your story has to remain consistent. If you're telling the truth, that shouldn't be a problem. Then the autopsy report has to come back from Raleigh. It hasn't been received yet, and that should tell a whole lot, possibly even what happened after you left Tydings standing by the koi pond. I hope I am correct about that. But I can tell you this; I believe you; and I will do my best to explain this to Lieutenant Davis, and the D.A. No doubt you will be taken into custody, but I will support you each step of the way. Trust me, we will see this through together. I and my beloved *Polite Society* are entitled to some good old fashioned apologies; and I am confident that when all the facts are in, you will be too."

"Stay here, let me go downstairs and get Lieutenant Davis. For the near term, he will be in charge of you, and I will be available if you need me. First and foremost we have to get you some good local legal representation."

Downstairs, the Lieutenant and Chris were chatting; the other guests were already off to dinner. I explained to them in some detail my conversation upstairs, and I was particularly pleased with Richard's very positive reaction. Chris let out a heartfelt sigh of relief. "I am so glad that this appears to be over," she murmured. "But now what?"

"Richard, Phil Kerry is waiting for you upstairs." I said. "Please let his wife accompany him every step of the way as far as possible. And also, please let me be involved in his defense wherever possible."

"I think you have nailed it, Ed. We still have a lot of questions to resolve, and need a more detailed explanation of events, but I think I have a good feeling about this. I think we just may have what we all want, a satisfactory resolution."

Lieutenant Davis, now my friend 'Richard', and the Kerrys left shortly thereafter. Richard did not handcuff Phil Kerry, and I was quite grateful for that. Barbara would return for their things in their guest room, and upon her return to Florida would unquestionably stay in touch. Chris offered to make a room available whenever she needed to be back in Asheville.

With them now gone, the inn was quiet and Chris and I sat together on the porch, each satisfied that, in our opinion, the truth had come out, and things around the inn could now return to normal.

"Whew," I said. "This has been some three days."

"May I congratulate you my dear," Chris said. "You handled this situation for the most part with great consideration. I am duly impressed."

"Why, thank you dear heart, your approval means a great deal to me." Then I chuckled and added: "You know how I dwell mightily on your approval."

Ah, there it was…. the old 'fish eye' from my girl, over the rim of a glass of her favorite single malt. At this point I was quite content to have the unfortunate events of the past few days behind us, and hopefully resolved. It was over. Thank goodness it was over. The inn was safe, my reputation should once again be intact, and my beloved Cohiba never tasted better.

Once again, tomorrow promised to be 'just another day in Paradise.' Let there be no more surprises!

CHAPTER XIV

Resolution....

A few days later

"I am not happy", grumbled Ed, "and I know that Richard feels like he was betrayed by his own people.

"Settle down, tiger," offered Chris, "your current attitude is really unpleasant. You know that our guests want to be titillated with details, and all you come up with is 'let's just wait for a completed investigation before jumping the gun'."

"I can't help it Chris, I feel like I let the Kerrys down."

"There is reason for concern, dear, I know that. In fact I did notice a slight degree of coolness from Barbara Kerry the last time we had our daily phone conversations."

"I can tell you, likewise, that Phillip is rapidly losing faith in 'the system'. But everyone else is so happy! The DA is really enjoying his '15 minutes of fame'. This reminds me so much of that infamous Duke Lacrosse fiasco. There must be something in the North Carolina D.A.s' bottled water supply. Our D.A. was so over the top on TV the other day, indicating he had found his man; the tragic homicide was resolved, even while admitting that certain evidence was still coming in. It's the same old, same old, everyone wanted a fall guy and a quick resolution and by God they got it."

"Enough!" Chris chastised me. "You'll have a heart attack."

"I know honey, the D.A. was very good to me when all this started, but his actions are so transparent now, at least to me anyway. He's up for re-election, and he'll do and say anything, and worse throw anyone under the campaign bus to get publicity. He sized up right away how much national news coverage this story attracted. Not to mention his currying favor with our Mayor and other civic and tourism leaders, including that of our own Bed and Breakfast Association. Hell, he even appeared at a downtown Rotary meeting yesterday, and spoke at length about his office's dogged investigation and the satisfaction that he felt about achieving the goals of this fair city. Rats! He's doing all this for the air time, and he has not a bit of compassion for the Kerry family. Everyone is just so relieved and proud of our darling D.A. and the police department."

"Ed, you know I can't stand sarcasm right now! I'm upset too! You know I feel as badly as you do. I worry myself to sleep at night; and have you ever seen this kitchen in such a mess. I can't keep up with myself."

"I'm going downstairs to my office, Chris. Maybe we should take a pass on this coming week for guests. We're not booked beyond the next two days yet; just tell everyone who calls that we're full and refer them to Jerry across the street."

I knew that using our accepted way of taking time for ourselves without "refusing" a guest would tip off Chris to how much I wanted to stick my head in the sand. So what? But she got on that right away.

"No way, mister! You get hold of yourself and straighten up; go play a round of golf, tell some ugly jokes at the club, and get yourself back into the swing of things. I continue to have a good feeling about things. Don't forget that Lieutenant Davis is still working on tracking down those issues you two discussed, and the autopsy report is still not here. Hang in there. Don't worry about the politicians; keep the faith. Something good is about to happen and I can feel it coming."

"Alright, alright, I hear you. It's just... Oh, never mind! I'm going down to keep a date with a fresh Monte Cristo."

There was little reason to question the city's reaction. Our little sordid event was resolved, it was an aberration of sorts, and surely left no stain on Asheville. 'Just out of town troublemakers, if you ask me'. Ha. So many people and businesses in our area relied heavily on tourism and its continued health; so what if one person had to be thrown under the bus for the good of all. I wanted to believe Chris; it really wasn't like her to pretend or entertain wishful thinking.

I lit up my cigar, leaned back and tried to think positive thoughts. As to be expected, most of the information I shared with Richard was now appearing in the press. Young Mr. Kerry did indeed have very strong motives for wishing Tydings harm, and he had an excellent opportunity. He admitted to being alone with the victim behind the bed and breakfast. It was frightening how quickly the case was built against Kerry, and how believable it was to the general public. Internally, little credit was given to Kerry's signed Visa receipt. The time stamp was clear but the date and day were not entirely legible. It was offered that the receipt could have been from the day before, or at least some other occasion. After all, who cares about evidence when an election is in sight?

I thought about how some word of my involvement had surfaced, and how I had received some lukewarm kudos from several of my supposed friends and colleagues. In a perverse way it delighted me to caution everyone that the investigation was still ongoing, and there were definitely some loose ends any dogged defense counsel would seize upon. This only served to exasperate each caller, and delight me even more.

My private line rang and I picked it up immediately. "Hello, Richard." "Hey, hold on, slow down, I can barely make out what you're saying."

"Ed, Ed, you won't believe this. I just got a copy of the autopsy report! You won't believe this!"

"Slow down! Get a grip and tell me what it says."

"It says that Tydings had a little known history of heart trouble. The official cause of death is a massive coronary! Ed, I read this as 'natural causes'. What do you think?"

"Well, offhand, I think you're right, Richard. This is good news."

"Ed, it gets even better, I think! But you know how it's gone so far with my 'thinking'! You know that bruise on Tydings cheek?" He didn't wait for my reply. "Because Tydings was on a blood thinner for his heart condition and bruised so easily it was determined to be inconsequential and had occurred some time before the coronary; also it was not due to his fall into the pond. According to the report, the bruise played no part in Tydings death."

"Not bad at all Richard, this is really good news!"

"Just hold on, Ed", his voice got quieter and slower and I got a knot in my stomach.

"I brought this right to the Chief, and while he quickly indicated that this appeared supportive of Kerry's story, he would have to get the D.A.'s take on it, before it went any further. I wasn't to let you or anyone else know until he got back to me from the D.A. As soon as he gets back and briefs me, I'll call officially. I had to let you know right away. Now, keep this under you hat, please."

I ran up the stairs to see Chris and brief her on Richard's call. She flew into my arms for a huge hug. "Now all I have to do", I told her, "is to figure out how to wait patiently for Richard's call back after the Chief sees the D.A. Tell me again that all will soon be well."

"Why don't you go out and weed the herb garden. Felicia's favorite spot is getting overgrown with the new ground cover you planted in the spring. You should be able to go near to the pond without getting a sinking feeling anymore –oops, no pun intended. As soon as the phone rings, I'll call you.

The weeding didn't distract me or make the time go any faster. I felt that the call from Richard would not come soon enough for me. Little did I know it would come much too soon.

"Ed, phone for you! It's Richard, but I can't read his voice. Something's up."

It was Richard, and he had lost his excitement.

"The Chief got back to me quickly, too quickly. The D.A. was totally unimpressed by the autopsy report. He just about shouted at the Chief that the report supported his contention that he could get a jury to see that the coronary was directly caused by the unprovoked sucker punch to Mr. Tydings head. He was adamant that there were grounds for manslaughter charges, and while the death was not premeditated, it was still of an evil, revengeful nature. The D.A. also told the Chief that the autopsy report was not to be released just yet. It has something to with the prosecution's strategy."

After a brief pause, during which I couldn't find any words to say, he continued, a little more hopefully.

"I think it's all a big bluff, Ed. The report also indicated that there was a tiny bit of pond water in Tydings lungs. He fell head first into the pond, while taking his last breath. This is an important report Ed, I can feel it."

Someone else with a good feeling, I thought.

"My God, I hope you're right about that. What happens now? Can we share any of this with Kerry? Or anyone else? Can we?"

"Not unless I personally go against the D.A.'s direct order. He told the Chief nothing was to be released, remember? You must hold off saying anything to Phillip yet. But as you should know, and I want you to remember this, I'm still working on some leads, and I'm waiting to hear on one further piece of evidence. I may hear back shortly on some phone logs. Let's stay in touch, and buck up kiddo."

This last statement caused me to smile. I was amused at how this surprising alliance with Richard was advancing to downright friendship. Feeling somewhat confused I went upstairs into the kitchen where Chris was completing her prepping for tomorrow's morning's breakfast.

"I'm not sure how I feel about that call. I just can't accept the D.A.'s motives in all this. The autopsy report should have generated some very serious questions about Kerry's responsibility. The D.A. continues to maintain that Kerry was right there and sucker punched Tydings into a coronary. But Richard doesn't seem to be deterred. He's got something up his sleeve. We'll just have to trust him."

Chris gave me one of her best reassuring looks and told me again, "I told you; I had a good feeling, and as Richard keeps digging there will be more good news. Now run across and get cleaned up for wine and cheese. I see the first car returning to the parking area."

Later that evening, Chris and I were sitting on the side porch, the guests were all out to dinner and we were enjoying as best we could, some good old 'downtime'. The phone rang and Chris moved to the kitchen to answer it. She returned.

"That was Richard, in a highly excited state. He just kept repeating that he had the bombshell, the final nail for the D.A.'s coffin, and he's on his way over."

Chris had barely stopped speaking when we heard a car in the parking area. We walked to the back, catching a good whiff of the sweet smell of Richard's cigarillos, and noted immediately his triumphant grin.

"I've got it! I've got it right here." He was waving around a stack of papers that glowed ghostly white in the light coming from the kitchen windows.

"Let's go inside, this is it, Ed, this is it."

We got comfortable and private in my den, and Richard took a deep breath and began telling his news.

"You folks both know that since the arrest and charges, I have been pursuing the records of Tydings cell phone. I didn't realize that so many new advances in technology have made it possible for anyone to trace a cell phone call. It used to be very difficult; the Police channels had special equipment that could tell you the general location of an AT&T or Bell Atlantic call. For the most part the impetus was the events of September eleventh. New on line technology has allowed specialized companies to buy private information from cellular carriers. Hell, there are even GPS elements in most cell phones."

Richard seemed to want us to realize that he had done some serious investigative work.

"I had to do all this on my own time, since the department and the D.A. considered the case solved and no extra hours needed to be expended on it. You had suggested this Ed, after that random statement by young Tydings at the ball field. Young Tydings told you that he had talked to his dad on Thursday at 9:45 AM; the elder Tydings telling him that he was fed up with "unprintable" you, and your *Polite Society*! I talked to the son after you mentioned that. He said that his father had only stayed here to get under your skin and treat you like an ill favored servant in front of your guests to embarrass you the way you'd embarrassed him by refusing to support him in his business ventures. But as of that call, Tydings Sr. was going to leave right away; you weren't rising to the bait like you should have. Young Tydings said he was sure of the time because he checked his watch, because he had a meeting at 11:00."

"Now, there's more. Tydings placed a call to the Richmond Hall Inn at 9:55AM! That is almost exactly the same time *we say* Phil Kerry was signing his VISA charge at a gas station in Biltmore Village *six miles away*! In his stack of papers, Richard produced a copy of Kerry's VISA record which clearly showed the date and time of the gas station charge, exactly as Kerry had maintained."

"Whoa." I interrupted him. "I need a minute to digest all this. This is getting really good."

I glanced happily at Chris who met my eyes in that unspoken and satisfied look of contentment that older couples achieve over the years. Were we turning into our parents, who communicated without speaking so much of the time?

"I have already interviewed, and have a signed statement from the clerk who took Tydings call, and he remembers it vividly," Richard continued.

"Tydings had called to push up by one day his reservation through the weekend. The clerk informed him that his lack of timely confirmation on the original reservation had caused his suite to be given to another party. Also, his new request for a room that night could not be accommodated because the Inn was full. The clerk remembered all too well the conversation. Tydings had not only threatened him with legal action, but also with personal bodily harm. The clerk reluctantly hung up on this potential guest with his supervisor's approval. Since hanging up on a person is very much against the Inn's policy, a record was made of the call and time stamped."

Richard looked at us. We didn't have to say anything for him to see clearly just how relieved and happy we were.

"Ed, I bounced all this off the Chief just before coming over here. He sized up the issues quickly, and admitted that perhaps several positions have to be backtracked, and that might prove difficult for some city leaders, however necessary."

"Oh, don't worry," I explained. "Most of those folks are experts on spinning any position around. In fact, it wouldn't surprise me to see the Chief and the D.A. now take credit for these revelations. But who cares, the important thing is that this, along with the autopsy should make Phil Kerry a free man!"

"Yeah" replied Richard, not too enthusiastically.

"I'm scheduled to meet with the Chief and the D.A. tomorrow morning. I feel good about laying this out for them. My guess is they'll spend some more time on seeking cover, or finding a way to spin this to their advantage."

Chris finally broke her silence. "Now, now, Richard, you did great work, we know it, the Kerrys will know it and I'm sure the Chief knows it. Let's just be thankful for the evidence and hope for a speedy resolution. Be cautioned however, nothing is set yet."

I smacked my thigh and let out a great big sigh of relief. And there he was, our friend Richard Davis, his legs now stretched out, leaning back in his chair, blowing smoke rings at the ceiling. Yes, indeed, he was feeling good, as well he should!

"All right folks." I said, "It's late and this camper has to lock up the front and then head over for my beauty sleep. I have to be bright and shiny, and witty and entertaining for our guests in the morning."

"Oh, please!" Chris burst out.

A few minutes later Chris and I wound up on the side porch again. It was only a couple of days ago that Chris and I sat here after watching Phil Kerry escorted by the good lieutenant leave for jail. Tonight we were both optimistic about the turn of events and Kerry's much reduced involvement. That last time we sat here we assured ourselves with half-hearted hope that "tomorrow has the bright promise to be just another day in Paradise! Please, let there be no more surprises." I now repeated that sentiment with great confidence, especially the 'no surprises' part.

And there proved to be none!!

Phil Kerry was released from custody the next day, with little to no fanfare. The evidence was overwhelming. All along we knew that Kerry did not have the resources or luxury to hire an expensive legal team and now he had no need to do so. In a hastily called news conference the D.A. explained that several avenues of investigation initiated by 'his office and the Police Department' had uncovered new evidence mitigating the suspect's alleged guilt, and he had no reason to hold Kerry any further. The entire episode was to be ruled a very tragic 'natural death from heart complications' and all parties were to move on accordingly. In his best officious manner he reminded the public that Asheville remained a very exciting and safe holiday and vacation destination.

Chris and I had no quarrel with this, and Phil and Barbara Kerry were now free to return home together to Florida. There were promises to return at another time to accept our gracious hospitality. The reputation of our beloved inn, *Polite Society,* was intact. Once again, at the conclusion of any breakfast, and after seeing the guests off for the day, I could return to nothing more exciting than my cup of hazelnut coffee, my crossword, and my favorite cigar.

EPILOGUE

Afterwards. ...

Polite Society continues to enjoy an excellent reputation as a favorite get away destination. The service at breakfast continues to be impeccable, and the inn clearly remains..."A Special Place!"

Polite Society remains a prominent feature on the 'Christmas Tour of Historic Homes'.

Page's husband Vince has had his company acquired by a firm from San Diego, California. Additional capital was provided and Vince was subsequently promoted to Vice President.

Dianna's fund raising efforts for United Way have improved dramatically from certain Florida companies.

The fund-raising brunches at *Polite Society* to benefit the Symphony Guild continue to be sell-outs.

Ed and Jerry prevailed later that same year to win first place in the team category at the Country Club.

The now 'Captain' Davis has become something of a regular off-duty visitor at the inn.

Ms. Temperance Bother, the beleaguered TV anchorwoman, was unceremoniously let go by the local station, her New York aspirations in bitter ashes. She has occasionally been seen doing appliance commercials for a local retailer.

The contract of Stan Eager, former President of the Asheville Chamber of Commerce was not renewed that fall. He was last heard from looking for a position in Iowa.

That year, Chris did some of her Christmas shopping early. A Deerstalker hat remains hidden away, ready for presentation at just the right moment.

AUTHOR'S BIOGRAPHY

Everett Colby spent over 25 years in corporate banking assignments in New York City and Miami. Upon Retirement he and his wife Ann established The Colby House, a Bed & Breakfast in Asheville, NC.

Now fully retired, Everett and Ann currently reside in Mars Hill, NC with their golden retriever, Reilly.